Truman Capote

SUMMER CROSSING

A NOVEL

Afterword by Alan U. Schwartz

 THE MODERN LIBRARY · NEW YORK

This is a work of fiction.
Names, characters, places, and incidents are the products of the author's imagination
or are used fictitiously. Any resemblance to actual events, locales, or persons,
living or dead, is entirely coincidental.

2006 Modern Library Paperback Edition

Published in the United States by Modern Library, an imprint of
The Random House Publishing Group, a division of
Random House, Inc., New York.

MODERN LIBRARY and the TORCHBEARER Design are registered trademarks of
Random House, Inc.

Originally published in hardcover in the United States by Random House, an imprint of
The Random House Publishing Group, a division of Random House, Inc., in 2005.

Library of Congress Cataloging-in-Publication Data
Capote, Truman
Summer crossing: a novel / Truman Capote.—1st ed.
p. cm.
ISBN 0-8129-7593-6
1. Manhattan (New York, N.Y.)—Fiction. I. Title.
PS3505.A59S86 2006
813'.54—dc22   2005054307

Printed in the United States of America

www.modernlibrary.com

6 8 9 7

Book design by Carole Lowenstein

Truman Capote

Truman Capote was born Truman Streckfus Persons on September 30, 1924, in New Orleans. His early years were affected by an unsettled family life. He was turned over to the care of his mother's family in Monroeville, Alabama; his father was imprisoned for fraud; his parents divorced and then fought a bitter custody battle over Truman. Eventually he moved to New York City to live with his mother and her second husband, a Cuban businessman whose name he adopted. The young Capote got a job as a copyboy at *The New Yorker* in the early forties, but was fired for inadvertently offending Robert Frost. The publication of his early stories in *Harper's Bazaar* established his literary reputation when he was in his twenties. His novel *Other Voices, Other Rooms* (1948), a Gothic coming-of-age story that Capote described as "an attempt to exorcise demons," and his novella *The Grass Harp* (1951), a gentler fantasy rooted in his Alabama years, consolidated his precocious fame.

From the start of his career Capote associated himself with a wide range of writers and artists, high-society figures, and international celebrities, gaining frequent media attention for his exuberant social life. He collected his stories in *A Tree of Night* (1949) and published the novella *Breakfast at Tiffany's* (1958), but devoted his energies increasingly to the stage—adapting *The Grass Harp* into a play and writing the musical *House of Flowers* (1954)—and to journalism, of which the earliest examples are "Local Color" (1950) and "The Muses Are Heard" (1956). He made a brief foray into the movies to write the screenplay for John Huston's *Beat the Devil* (1954).

Capote's interest in the murder of a family in Kansas led to the prolonged investigation that provided the basis for *In Cold Blood* (1966), his most successful and acclaimed book. By "treating a real event with fictional techniques," Capote intended to create a new synthesis: something both "immaculately factual" and a work of art. However its genre was defined, from the moment it began to appear in serialized form in *The New Yorker* the book exerted a fascination among a wider readership than Capote's writing had ever attracted

BOOKS BY TRUMAN CAPOTE

Other Voices, Other Rooms
A Tree of Night
Local Color
The Grass Harp
The Muses Are Heard
Breakfast at Tiffany's
Observations (with Richard Avedon)
Selected Writings
In Cold Blood
A Christmas Memory
The Thanksgiving Visitor
The Dogs Bark
Music for Chameleons
One Christmas
Three by Truman Capote
Answered Prayers: The Unfinished Novel
A Capote Reader
The Complete Stories of Truman Capote
Too Brief a Treat: The Letters of Truman Capote
(edited by Gerald Clarke)

SUMMER CROSSING

before. The abundantly publicized masked ball at the Plaza Hotel with which he celebrated the completion of *In Cold Blood* was an iconic event of the 1960s, and for a time Capote was a constant presence on television and in magazines, even trying his hand at movie acting in *Murder by Death*.

He worked for many years on *Answered Prayers*, an ultimately unfinished novel that was intended to be the distillation of everything he had observed in his life among the rich and famous; an excerpt from it published in *Esquire* in 1975 appalled many of Capote's wealthy friends for its revelation of intimate secrets, and he found himself excluded from the world he had once dominated. In his later years he published two collections of fiction and essays, *The Dogs Bark* (1973) and *Music for Chameleons* (1980). He died on August 25, 1984, after years of problems with drugs and alcohol.

The Complete Stories of Truman Capote and *Too Brief a Treat: The Letters of Truman Capote* were published in 2004.

SUMMER CROSSING

Chapter 1

"You are a mystery, my dear," her mother said, and Grady, gazing across the table through a centerpiece of roses and fern, smiled indulgently: yes, I am a mystery, and it pleased her to think so. But Apple, eight years older, married, far from mysterious, said: "Grady is only foolish; I wish I were going with you. Imagine, Mama, this time next week you'll be having breakfast in Paris! George keeps promising that we'll go . . . I don't know, though." She paused and looked at her sister. "Grady, why on earth do you want to stay in New York in the dead of summer?" Grady wished they would leave her alone; still this harping, and here now was the very morning the boat sailed: what was there to say beyond what she'd said? After that there was only the truth, and the truth she did not entirely intend to tell. "I've never spent a summer here," she said, escaping their eyes and look-ing out the window: the dazzle of traffic heightened the June morning quiet of Central Park, and the sun, full of first sum-mer, that dries the green crust of spring, plunged through the trees fronting the Plaza, where they were breakfasting. "I'm perverse; have it your own way." She realized with a smile it was perhaps a mistake to have said that: her family did come rather near thinking her perverse; and once when she was fourteen she'd had a terrible and quite acute insight: her mother, she saw, loved her without really liking her; she had thought at first that this was because her mother considered her plainer, more obstinate, less playful than Apple, but later, when it was apparent, and painfully so to Apple, that Grady was finer looking by far, then she gave up reasoning about her mother's viewpoint: the answer of course, and at last she saw this too, was simply that in an inactive sort of way, she'd never, not even as a very small girl, much liked her mother. Yet there was little flamboyancy in either attitude; indeed, the house of their hostility was modestly furnished with affec-tion, which Mrs. McNeil now expressed by closing her daughter's hand in her own and saying: "We *will* worry about you, darling. We can't help that. I don't know. I don't know. I'm not sure it's safe. Seventeen isn't very old, and you've never been really alone before."

Mr. McNeil, who whenever he spoke sounded as though he was bidding in a poker game, but who seldom spoke in any event, partly because his wife did not like to be interrupted and partly because he was a very tired man, dunked out a cigar in his coffee cup, causing both Apple and Mrs. McNeil to wince, and said: "When I was eighteen, why hell, I'd been out in California three years."

"But after all, Lamont . . . you're a man."

"What's the difference?" he grunted. "There has been no difference between men and women for some while. You say so yourself."

As though the conversation had taken an unpleasant turn, Mrs. McNeil cleared her throat. "It remains, Lamont, that I am very uneasy in leaving—"

Rising inside Grady was an ungovernable laughter, a joyous agitation which made the white summer stretching before her seem like an unrolling canvas on which she might draw those first rude pure strokes that are free. Then, too, and with a straight face, she was laughing because there was so little they suspected, nothing. The light quivering against the table silver seemed to at once encourage her excitement and to flash a warning signal: careful, dear. But elsewhere something said Grady, be proud, you are tall so fly your pennant high above and in the wind. What could have spoken, the rose? Roses speak, they are the hearts of wisdom, she'd read so somewhere. She looked out the window again; the laughter was flowing up, it was flooding on her lips: what a sparkling sun-slapped day for Grady McNeil and roses that speak!

"Why is that so funny, Grady?" Apple did not have a pleasant voice; it suggested the subvocal prattlings of an ill-natured baby. "Mother asks a simple question, and you laugh as though she were an idiot."

"Grady doesn't think me an idiot, surely not," said Mrs. McNeil, but a tone of weak conviction indicated doubt, and her eyes, webbed by the spidery hat-veil she now lowered over her face, were dimly confused with the sting she always felt when confronted by what she considered Grady's contempt. It was all very well that between them there should be only the thinnest contact: there was no real sympathy, she knew that; still, that Grady by her remoteness could suggest herself superior was unendurable: in such moments Mrs. McNeil's hands twitched. Once, but this had been a great many years ago and when Grady was still a tomboy with chopped hair and scaly knees, she had not been able to control them, her hands, and on that occasion, which of course was during that period which is the most nervously trying of a woman's life, she had, provoked by Grady's inconsiderate aloofness, slapped her daughter fiercely. Whenever she'd known afterwards similar impulses she steadied her hands on some solid surface, for, at the time of her previous unrestraint, Grady, whose green estimating eyes were like scraps of sea, had stared her down, had stared through her and turned a searchlight on the spoiled mirror of her vanities: because she was a limited woman, it was her first experience with a will-power harder than her own. "Surely not," she said, twinkling with artificial humor.

"I'm sorry," said Grady. "Did you ask a question? I never seem to hear anymore." She intended the last not so much as an apology as a serious confession.

"Really," twittered Apple, "one would think you were in love."

There was a knocking at her heart, a sense of danger, the silver shook momentously, and a lemon-wheel, half-squeezed in Grady's finger, paused still: she glanced swiftly into her sister's eyes to see if anything were there that was more shrewd than stupid. Satisfied, she finished squeezing the lemon into her tea and heard her mother say: "It is about the dress, dear. I think I may as well have it made in Paris: Dior or Fath, someone like that. It might even be less expensive in the long run. A soft leaf green would be heaven, especially with your coloring and hair—though I must say I wish you wouldn't cut it so short: it seems unsuitable and not—not quite feminine. A pity debutantes can't wear green. Now I think something in white watered silk—"

Grady interrupted her with a frown. "If this is the party dress, I don't want it. I don't want a party, and I don't intend to go to any, not those kind at any rate. I will not be made a fool."

Of all the things that fatigued her, this tried and annoyed Mrs. McNeil most: she trembled as if unnatural vibrations jarred the sane and stable precincts of the Plaza dining-room. Nor do I mean to be made a fool, she might have said, for, in contemplating the promotion of Grady's debut year, she'd done already a great lot of work, maneuvering: there was even some idea of hiring a secretary. Furthermore, and in a self-righteous vein, she could have gone even so far as to say that the whole of her social life, every drab luncheon and tiresome tea (as in this light she would describe them), had been suffered only in order that her daughters receive a dazzling acceptance in the years of their dance. Lucy McNeil's own debut had been a famous and sentimental affair: her grandmother, a rightfully celebrated New Orleans beauty who had married South Carolina's Senator LaTrotta, presented Lucy and her two sisters en masse at a Camellia ball in Charleston in April of 1920; it was a presentation truly, for the three

LaTrotta sisters were no more than schoolgirls whose social adventures had been heretofore conducted within the shackles of a church; so hungrily had Lucy whirled that night her feet for days had worn the bruises of this entrance into living, so hungrily had she kissed the Governor's son that her cheeks had flamed a month in remorseful shame, for her sisters—spinsters then and spinsters still—claimed kissing made babies: no, her grandmother said, hearing her teary confession, kissing does not make babies—neither does it make ladies. Relieved, she continued through to a year of triumph; it was a triumph because she was pleasant to look at, not unbearable to listen to: vast advantages when you remember that this was the meager season when the junior assembly had only such deplorable persimmons to choose among as Hazel Veere Numland or the Lincoln girls. Then, too, during the winter holidays, her mother's family, they were the Fairmonts from New York, had given in her honor, and in this very hotel, the Plaza, a distinguished dance; even though she sat now so near the scene, and was trying to recall, there was little about it she could remember, except that it was all gold and white, that she'd worn her mother's pearls, and, oh yes, she'd met Lamont McNeil, an unremarkable event: she danced with him once and thought nothing of it. Her mother, however, was more impressed, for Lamont McNeil, while socially unknown, and though still in his late twenties, cast over Wall Street an ever enlarging shadow, and so was considered a catch, if not in the circle of angels, then by those of a but slightly lower stratum. He was asked to dinner. Lucy's father invited him to South Carolina for the duck-shoot. *Manly*, old grand Mrs. LaTrotta commented, and, as this was her criterion, she gave him the golden seal. Seven months later Lamont McNeil, pitching his poker voice to its tenderest tremor, spoke his piece, and Lucy, having received only two other proposals, one absurd and the second a jest, said oh Lamont I'm the happiest girl in the world. She was nineteen when she had her first child: Apple, so named, amusingly enough, because during her pregnancy Lucy McNeil had eaten them by the barrel, but her grandmother, appearing at the christening, thought it a shocking bit of frivolity—jazz and the twenties, she said, had gone to Lucy's head. But this choice of name was the last gay exclamation point to a protracted childhood, for a year later she lost her second baby; stillborn, it was a son, and she called him Grady in memory of her brother killed in the war. She brooded a long while, Lamont hired a yacht and they cruised the Mediterranean; at every bright pastel port, from St. Tropez to Taormina, she gave on board sad weeping ice-cream parties for gangs of embarrassed native boys the steward shanghaied from ashore. But on their return to

America, this tearful mist abruptly lifted: she discovered the Red Cross, Harlem, the two-demand bid, she took a professional interest in Trinity Church, the Cosmopolitan, the Republican Party, there was nothing she would not sponsor, contribute to, connive for: some said she was admirable, others said brave, a few despised her. They made a spirited clique, however, these few, and over the years their combined strength had sabotaged a dozen of her ambitions. Lucy had waited; she had waited for Apple: the mother of a topflight debutante has at her hands a social version of atomic revenge; but then she was cheated out of it, for there was the new war, and the poor taste of a debut in wartime would have been excessive: they had instead given an ambulance to England. And now Grady was trying to cheat her, too. Her hands twitted on the table, flew to the lapel of her suit, plucked at a brooch of cinnamon diamonds: it was too much, Grady had tried always to cheat her, just simply by not having been born a boy. She'd named her Grady anyway, and poor Mrs. LaTrotta, then in the last exasperated year of her life, had roused herself sufficiently to declare Lucy morbid. But Grady had never been Grady, not the child she wanted. And it was not that in this matter Grady wanted to be ideal: Apple, with her pretty playful ways and aided by Lucy's sense of style, would have been an assured success, but Grady, who, for one thing, seemed not

popular with young people, was a gambling chance. If she refused to cooperate, failure was certain. "There *will* be a debut,
Grady McNeil," she said, stretching her gloves. "You will
wear white silk and carry a bouquet of green orchids: it will
catch a little the color of your eyes and your red hair. And we
will have that orchestra the Bells had for Harriet. I warn you
now, Grady, if you behave rottenly about this I shall never
speak to you again. Lamont, will you ask for the check,
please?"

Grady was silent some moments; she knew the others
were not as calm as they seemed: they were waiting again for
her to act up, which proved with what inaccuracy they observed her, how unaware they were of her recent nature. A
month ago, two months ago, if she had felt her dignity so in-
truded upon, she would have rushed out and roared her car
onto the port road with the pedal flat on the floor; she would
have found Peter Bell and cut the mischief in some highway
tavern; she would have made them worry. But what she felt
now was a genuine disinvolvement. And to some extent a
sympathy with Lucy's ambitions. It was so far off, a summer
away; there was no reason to believe it would ever happen, a
white silk dress, and the orchestra the Bells had had for Harriet. While Mr. McNeil paid the check, and as they crossed
the dining-room, she held Lucy's arm and with a coltish

awkwardness gave her cheek a delicate spontaneous peck. It was a gesture that had the sudden effect of unifying them all; they were a family: Lucy glowed, her husband, her daughters, she was a proud woman, and Grady, for all her stubborn oddness was, let anyone say whatever they would, a wonderful child, a real person. "Darling," Lucy said, "I'm going to miss you."

Apple, who was walking ahead, turned around. "Did you drive your car in this morning, Grady?"

Grady was slow in answering; lately everything Apple said seemed suspicious; why care, really? What if Apple did know? Still, she did not want her to. "I took the train from Greenwich."

"Then you left the car at home?"

"Why, does it make any difference?"

"No; well, yes. And you needn't bark at me. I only thought you could drive me out on the Island. I promised George I'd stop by the apartment and pick up his encyclopedia—such a heavy thing. I'd hate to carry it on the train. If we got there early enough you could go swimming."

"Sorry, Apple. The car's in a garage; I left it here the other day because the speedometer got jammed. I suppose it's ready now, but as a matter of fact I have a date in town."

"Oh?" said Apple peevishly. "Mind if I ask who with?"

Grady minded very much, but "Peter Bell," she answered.

"Peter Bell, good Lord, why do you always see him? He thinks he's so smart."

"He is."

"Apple," Lucy said, "Grady's friends are no concern of yours. Peter is a charming boy; and his mother was one of my bridesmaids. Lamont, do you remember? She caught the bouquet. But isn't Peter still up in Cambridge?"

Just then Grady heard her name shouted across the lobby: "Hiho, McNeil!" Only one person in the world called her that, and with an imitated delight, for it was not the happiest time he could have chosen to appear, she saw that it was him. A young man expensively but perversely dressed (he wore a white evening tie with a severe flannel suit, the trousers of which were held up by a wild-west belt of jeweled inappropriateness, and on his feet there were a pair of tennis sneakers), he was pocketing change at the cigar counter. As he went toward her, she going half-way to meet him, he walked with the easy grace of one who expects always to know the best things of life. "Aren't you pretty, McNeil?" he said, and gave her a confident hug. "But not as pretty as me: I've just been to the barber shop." The impeccable freshness of his clean neat-featured face showed as much; and a fresh haircut lent him that look of defenseless innocence that only a haircut can.

Grady gave him a happy tomboy shove. "Why aren't you in Cambridge? Or is the law too boring?"

"Boring, but not so boring as my family are going to be when they hear I've been booted out."

"I don't believe you," Grady laughed. "Anyway, I want to hear all about it. Only now we're in the most terrible rush. Mother and Dad are sailing for Europe, and I'm seeing them off on the boat."

"Can't I come, too? Please, miss?"

Grady hesitated, then called, "Apple, tell Mother Peter's coming with us," and Peter Bell, thumbing his nose at Apple behind her back, ran into the street to signal a taxi.

They needed two taxis; Grady and Peter, who waited to re-trieve from the cloakroom Lucy's little cross-eyed dachs-hund, used the second. It had a sky-window roof: dove flights, clouds and towers tumbled upon them; the sun, shooting summer-tipped arrows, jingled the new-penny color of Grady's cropped hair, and her skinny, nimble face, shaped with bones of fish-spine delicacy, was flushed by the honeyed blowing light. "If anyone should ask," she said, lighting Peter's cigarette for him, "Apple or anyone, do please say that we have a date."

"Is this a new trick, lighting gentlemen's cigarettes? And that lighter; McNeil, however did you come by it? Atrocious."

It was, rather. However, she'd never thought so until this moment. Made of mirror, and with an enormous sequined initial, it was the sort of novelty found on drugstore counters. "I bought it," she said. "It works wonderfully. Anyway, what I just said, you will remember?"

"No, my love, you never bought that. You try awfully hard, but I'm afraid you're not really very vulgar."

"Peter, are you teasing me?"

"Of course I am," he laughed, and she pulled his hair, laughing too. Though unrelated, Grady and Peter, they still were relatives, not through blood but out of sympathy: it was the happiest friendship she knew, and always with him she relaxed in the secure warm bath of it. "Why shouldn't I tease you? Isn't that what you're doing to me? No, no don't shake your head. You're up to something, and you're not going to tell me. Never mind, dear, I won't pester you now. As for the date, why not? Anything to evade my anguished parents. Only you'll damn well pay for it: after all, what's the point in spending money on you? I'd prefer trotting around dear sister

Harriet; she at least can tell you all about astronomy. By the way, do you know what that dreary girl has done: she's gone to Nantucket to spend the summer studying stars. Is that the boat? The *Queen Mary*? And I'd so hoped for something amusing like a Polish tanker. Whoever dreamed up that bilious whale ought to be gassed: you Irish are perfectly right, the English are horrors. But then, so are the French. The *Normandie* didn't burn soon enough. Even so, I wouldn't go on an American boat if you gave me—"

The McNeils were on A deck in a suite of varnished rooms with fake fireplaces. Lucy, just-arrived orchids trembling on her lapel, skittered to and fro while Apple trailed after her reading aloud from cards that had come with offerings of flowers and fruit. Mr. McNeil's secretary, the stately Miss Seed, passed among them with a Piper-Heidsieck bottle, her expression vaguely curled with the incongruity of champagne in the morning (Peter Bell told her not to bother with a glass, he would take whatever was left of the bottle), and Mr. McNeil himself, solemnly flattered, stood at the door discouraging a man who televised important travelers: "Sorry, old man . . . forgot my makeup ha ha." No one even liked Mr. McNeil's jokes except other men and Miss Seed: and that, so Lucy said, was only because Miss Seed was in love with him. The dachshund ripped the stockings of a fe-

male photographer who flashed Lucy in her rigidest ro-
togravure stance: "What are we planning to do abroad?"
said Lucy, repeating the reporter's query. "Why, I'm not
sure. We have a home in Cannes that we haven't seen since
the war; I suppose we'll stop by there. And shop; of course
we'll shop." She hemmed embarrassedly. "But mostly it's
the boat ride. There's nothing to change the spirit like a
summer crossing."

Stealing the champagne, Peter Bell led Grady away and
up through the saloons and onto an open deck where voy-
agers, parading with their well-wishers against the city skyline, had already proud ocean-roll walks. One lone child
stood at the railing forlornly flying kites of confetti: Peter offered him a swallow of champagne, but the child's mother, a
giant of uncommon physique, advanced with thunderous
steps and sent them fleeing to the dog-kennel deck. "Oh
dear," said Peter, "the dog house: isn't that always our lot."
They huddled together in a spot of sun; it was as hidden as a
stowaway's retreat, a yearning bellow from the smokestacks
poignantly baled away, and Peter said how wonderful it
would be if they could fall asleep and awake with stars overhead and the ship far at sea. Together, running on Connecticut shores and looking over the Sound, they had, years
before, spent whole days contriving elaborate and desperate

plots: Peter had assumed always a serious enthusiasm, he'd seemed absolutely to believe a rubber raft would float them to Spain, and something of that old note shivered his voice now. "I suppose it's just as well we're not children any-more," he said, dividing the last of the wine between them. "That really was too wretched. But I wish we were still chil-dren enough to stay on this boat."

Grady, stretching her brown naked legs, tossed her head. "I would swim ashore."

"Maybe I'm not up on you as I used to be. I've been away so much. But how could you turn down Europe, McNeil? Or is that rude? I mean, am I intruding on your secret?"

"There isn't a secret," she said, partly aggravated, partly enlivened with the knowledge that perhaps there was. "Not a real one. It's more, well, a privacy, a small privacy I should like to keep awhile longer, oh not always, but a week, a day, simply a few hours: you know, like a present you keep hidden in a drawer: it will be given away soon enough, but for a while you want it all to yourself." Though she had expressed her feeling inexpertly, she glanced at Peter's face, sure of see-ing there a reflection of his inveterate understanding; but she found only an alarming absence of expression: he seemed faded out, as though the sudden exposure to sun had drained him of all color, and, aware presently that he'd heard nothing she had said, she tapped him on the shoulder. "I was wondering," he said, blinking his eyes, "I was wondering if there is, after all, a final reward in unpopularity?"

It was a question with some history; but Grady, who had learned the answer from Peter's own life, was surprised, even a little shocked to hear him ask it so wistfully and, indeed, ask it at all. Peter had never been popular, it was true, not at school or at the club, not with any of the people they were, as he put it, condemned to know; and yet it was this very condition which had so sworn them together, for Grady, who cared not one way or the other, loved Peter, and had joined him in his outside realm quite as though she belonged there for the same reason he did: Peter, to be sure, had taught her that she was no more liked than himself: they were too fine, it was not their moment, this era of the adolescent, their appreciation he said would come at a future time. Grady had never bothered about it; in that sense, she saw, thinking back over what seemed now a ridiculous problem, she'd never been unpopular: it was just that she'd never made an effort, not felt deeply that to be liked was of importance. Whereas Peter had cared exceedingly. All their childhood she'd helped her friend build, drafty though it was, a sandcastle of protection. Such castles should deteriorate of natural and happy processes. That for Peter his should still exist was simply extraordinary. Grady, though she still had use for their file of privately humorous references, for the sad anecdotes and tender coinages they shared, wanted no part of the castle: that applauded hour, the golden moment Peter had promised, did he not know that it was now?

"I know," he said, as if, having divined this thought of hers, he now replied to it. "Nevertheless." I know. Nevertheless. He sighed over his motto. "I suppose you imagined I was joking. About the university. Really, I was kicked out; not for saying the wrong thing, but for saying perhaps the too-right thing: both would appear to be objectionable." The exuberant quality that so suited him rearranged his mischief-maker face. "I'm glad about you," he said inexplicably, but with such a waterfall of warmth that Grady pressed her cheek near his. "If I said that I was in love with you, that would be incestuous, wouldn't it, McNeil?" All-ashore gongs were clanging through the ship, and ashes of shadow, spilt by sudden cloud-shades, heaped the deck. Grady for an instant felt the oddest loss: poor Peter, he knew her even less, she realized, than Apple, and yet, because he was her only friend, she wanted to tell him: not now, sometime. And what would he say? Because he was Peter, she trusted him to love her more: if not, then let the sea usurp their castle, not the one they'd built to keep life out, it was already gone, at least for her, but another, that one sheltering friendships and promises.

As the sun flooded out, he stood up and pulled her to her feet, saying, "And where shall we be gala tonight?" but Grady, who every moment meant to explain that she could not keep a date with him, let it pass again, for, as they descended the steps, a steward, brassy with the shininess of a gong, called his warning to them, and later, confronted with the activity of Lucy's farewell, she forgot altogether.

Fanfaring a handkerchief, and embracing her daughters fitfully, Lucy followed them to the gangplank; once she'd seen them down the canvas tunnel, she hurried out on the deck and watched for their appearance beyond the green fence; when she saw them, all clustered together and gazing dazedly, she started flagging the handkerchief to show them where she was, but her arm grew strangely weak and, overtaken by a guilty sensation of incompleteness, of having left something unfinished, undone, she let it fall to her side. The handkerchief came to her eyes in earnest, and the image of Grady (she loved her! Before God she had loved Grady as much as the child would let her) bubbled in the blur; there were stricken days, difficult days, and though Grady was as different from her as she had been from her own mother, head-sure and harder, she still was not a woman, but a girl, a child, and it was a terrible mistake, they could not leave her here, she could not leave her child unfinished, incomplete, she would have to hurry, she would have to tell Lamont they mustn't go. But before she could move he had closed his arms around her; he was waving down to the children; and then she was waving too.

Chapter 2

Broadway is a street; it is also a neighborhood, an atmosphere. From the time she was thirteen, and during all those winters at Miss Risdale's classes, Grady had made, even if it meant skipping school, as it often did, secret and weekly expeditions into this atmosphere, the attraction at first being band-shows at the Paramount, the Strand, curious movies that never played the theaters east of Fifth or in Stamford and Greenwich. In the last year, however, she had liked only to walk around or stand on street-corners with crowds moving about her. She would stay all afternoon and sometimes until it was dark. But it was never dark there: the lights that had been running all day grew yellow at dusk, white at night, and the faces, those dream-trapped faces, revealed their most to her then. Anonymity was part of the pleasure, but while she was no longer Grady McNeil, she did not know who it was that replaced her, and the tallest fires of her excitement burned with a fuel she could not name. She never mentioned it to anyone, those pearl-eyed perfumed Negroes, those men, silk- or sailor-shirted, toughs or pale-toothed and lavender-suited, those men that watched, smiled, followed: which way are you going? Some faces, like the lady who changed money at Nick's Amusements, are faces that belong nowhere, are green shadows under green eyeshades, evening effigies embalmed and floating in the caramel-sweet air. Hurry. Doorway megaphones, frenziedly hurling into the glare sad roars of rhythm, accelerate the senses to collapse: run—out of the white into the real, the sexless, the jazzless, the joyful dark: these infatuating terrors she had told to no one.

On a side street off Broadway and not far from the Roxy Theatre there was an open-air parking lot. A lonesome, wasted-looking area, it lay there the only substantial sight on a block of popcorn emporiums and turtle shops. There was a sign at the entrance which said NEMO PARKING. It was expensive, and altogether inconvenient, but earlier in the year, after the McNeils had closed their apartment and opened the house in Connecticut, Grady had started leaving her car there whenever she drove into town.

Sometime in April a young man had come to work at the parking lot. His name was Clyde Manzer.

Before Grady reached the parking lot she was already look-ing for him: on dull mornings he occasionally wandered around in the neighborhood or sat in a local Automat drink-ing coffee. But he was nowhere to be seen; nor did she find him when she reached the lot itself. It was noon and a hot smell of gasoline came off the gravel. Though obviously he was not there she crossed the lot calling his name impa-tiently; the relief of Lucy's sailing, the year or hour she had waited to see him, all the things that had buoyed her through the morning seemed at once to have fallen out from under her; she finally gave up and stood quietly despondent in the throbbing glare. Then she remembered that sometimes he took naps in one of the cars.

Her own car, a blue Buick convertible with her initials on the Connecticut license-plate, was the last in line, and while she was still searching several cars away she realized she was going to find him there. He was asleep in the backseat. Al-though the top was lowered, she had not seen him before because he was scrunched down out of view. The radio hummed faintly with news of the day, and there was a detec-tive story open on his lap. Of many magics, one is watching a beloved sleep: free of eyes and awareness, you for a sweet moment hold the heart of him; helpless, he is then all, and however irrationally, you have trusted him to be, man-pure, child-tender. Grady leaned, looking over him, her hair falling a little in her eyes. The young man she looked at, he was somebody of about twenty-three, was neither handsome nor homely; indeed, it would have been difficult to walk in New York and not see reminders of him every few steps, although, being out in the open all day, he was very much more weathered than most. But there was an air of well-built suppleness about him, and his hair, black with small curls, fit him like a neat cap of Persian lamb. His nose was slightly broken, and this gave his face, which, with its rustic flush, was not without a certain quick-witted force, an exaggerated virility. His eyelids trembled, and Grady, feeling the heart of him slip through her fingers, tensed for their opening. "Clyde," she whispered.

He was not the first lover she had known. Two years before, when she was sixteen and had first had the car, she had driven around in Connecticut a reserved young couple from New York who were looking for a house. By the time they found the house, a small nice one on the grounds of a country club and side by side with a little lake, this couple, the Boltons,

were devoted to her, and Grady, for her part, seemed ob-
sessed: she supervised the moving, she made their rock-
garden, found them a servant, and on Saturdays she played
golf with Steve or helped him mow the lawn: Janet Bolton, a
reserved harmless pretty girl directly out of Bryn Mawr, was
five months pregnant and so disinclined toward the strenu-
ous. Steve was a lawyer, and, as he was with a firm that did
business with her father, the Boltons were often asked to Old
Tree, the name with which the McNeils had dignified their
acreage: Steve used the pool there, and the tennis courts, and
there was a home that had belonged to Apple that Mr. McNeil
gave him more or less on his own. Peter Bell was rather non-
plussed; and so were Grady's few other friends, for she saw
only the Boltons, or, to her way of thinking, she saw only
Steve; and, although all the time they spent together was not
sufficient, she took now and then to riding his commuter's
train with him into the city: waiting to take the train home
with him in the evening she wandered from one Broadway
movie to another. But there was no peace for her; she could
not understand why that first joy she had felt should have
turned to pain and now to misery. He knew. She was certain
that he knew; his eyes, watching her as she crossed a room, as
she swam toward him in the pool, those eyes knew and were
not displeased: so, along with her love, she learned some-

thing of hate, for Steve Bolton knew, and would do nothing to help her. It was then that every day was contrary, a treading down of ants, a pinching of firefly wings, rages, so it seemed, against all that was as helpless as her helpless and despised self. And she took to wearing the thinnest dresses she could buy, dresses so thin that every leaf-shadow or wind-ripple was a coolness that stroked her; but she would not eat, she liked only to drink Coca-Cola and smoke cigarettes and drive her car, and she became so flat and skinny that the thin dresses blew all around her.

Steve Bolton was in the habit of taking a swim before breakfast in the little lake beside his house, and Grady, who had discovered this, could not get it out of her head: she awoke mornings imagining him at the edge of the lake standing among the water reeds like a strange dawn gold bird. One morning she went there. A small pine grove grew near the lake and it was here that she hid herself, lying flat on the dew-damp needles. A gloom of autumn mist drifted on the lake: of course he was not coming, she had waited too long, summer had gone without her even noticing. Then she saw him on the path: casual, whistling, a cigarette in one hand, a towel in the other; he was wearing only a dressing-gown, which, when he reached the lake, he pulled off and threw on a rock. It was as though at last her star had fallen, one that, striking earth, turned not black but burned more bluely still: half-kneeling now, her arms lifted outward, as if to touch, to salute him while he waded there growing fairy-tale tall, it seemed, and lengthening toward her until, with the barest warning, he sank into the deep below the reeds: Grady, a cry escaping despite everything, slipped back against a tree, embracing it as though it were some portion of his love, some part of his splendor.

Janet Bolton's baby was born at the end of the season: the autumn, pheasant-speckled week before the McNeils closed Old Tree and moved back to their winter quarters in town. Janet Bolton was pretty desperate; she had almost lost the baby twice, and her nurse, after winning some sort of dance contest, had become increasingly irreverent: most of the time she didn't bother with appearing, so, if it had not been for Grady, Janet would not have known what to do. Grady would come over and make a little lunch and give the house a quick dust; there was one duty she approached always with elation: that is, she liked to collect Steve's laundry and hang up his clothes. The day the baby was born Grady found Janet doubled up and screaming. Whenever she had reason to be, Grady was always surprised at how fondly concerned her feelings for Janet actually were: a trifle of a person, like a seashell that might be picked up and, because of its pink frilled perfection, kept to admire but never put among a collector's serious treasures: unimportance was both her charm and her protection, for it was impossible to feel, as Grady certainly didn't, threatened by or jealous of her. But on the morning that Grady walked in and heard her screaming she felt a satisfaction which, while not meant to be cruel, at least prevented her from going at once to give aid, for it was as if all the torments she herself knew were triumphantly transposed into expression by these moments of Janet Bolton's agony. When at length she brought herself to do the necessary things she did them very well; she called the doctor, took Janet to the hospital, then rang up Steve in New York.

He came out on the next train; it was an uneasy afternoon they spent together at the hospital; night came, and still no word, and Steve, who had managed with Grady a few jokes, a game of hearts, withdrew to a corner and let silence settle between them. The stale despair of train-schedules, and business and bills to be paid, seemed to rise off him like tired dust, and he sat there blowing smoke rings, zeros hollow as Grady had begun to feel . . . it was as if she curved away from him into space, as if the lake-image of him receded before her until now she could see him actually, a view that struck her as the most moving of any, for, with the exhausted droop of his shoulders and the tear at the corner of his eye, he belonged to

Janet and to her child. Wanting to show her love for him, not
as a lover but as a man slumped with love and birth, she
moved toward him. A nurse had come to the doorway; and
Steve Bolton heard of his son without any change of expression. Slowly he climbed to his feet, his eyes blind-pale; and
with a sigh that swayed the room his head fell forward on
Grady's shoulder: I'm a very happy man, he said. It was done
then, there was nothing more she wanted of him, summer's
desires had fallen to winter seed: winds blew them far before
another April broke their flower.

"Come on, light me a cigarette." Clyde Manzer's voice,
grouchy with sleep, but always fairly hoarse and furry, had
some singular quality: it was easy to get an impression of
whatever he said, for there was a mumbling power, subdued
as a throttle left running, that dragged the slow-fuse of male-
ness through every syllable; nevertheless, he stumbled over
words, pauses occasionally so separating sentences that all
sense evaporated. "Don't nigger-lip it, kid. You always
nigger-lip." The voice, though attractive in its way, could be
misleading: because of it, some people thought him stupid:
this proved them simply unobservant: Clyde Manzer was not
in the least stupid: his particular smartness was, in fact, the

plainly obvious. The four-lettered scholarship that carries a diploma in know-how—how to run, where to hide, how to ride the subway and see a movie and use a pay-phone all without paying—these knowledges that come with a city childhood of block warfare and desperate afternoons when only the cruel and clever, the swift, the brave survive—was the training that gave his eyes their agile intensity. "Aw, you nigger-lipped it. Christ, I knew you would."

"I'll smoke it," Grady said; and, using the lighter Peter had thought so vulgar, she lighted him another. One Monday, which was Clyde's day off, they had gone to a shooting gallery and he had won the lighter there and given it to her: since then she liked lighting everybody's cigarettes: there was an excitement in seeing her secret, disguised as thin fire, leap naked between herself, who knew, and someone else, who might discover.

"Thanks, kid," he said, accepting the new cigarette. "You're a good kid: you didn't nigger-lip it. I'm just in a lousy mood, that's all. I shouldn't ought to sleep like that. I was having dreams."

"I hope I was in them."

"I don't remember nothing I dream," he said, rubbing his chin as though he needed a shave. "So tell me, did you get them off, your folks?"

"Just now—Apple wanted me to drive her home, and an old friend showed up: it was very confused, I came straight from the pier."

"There's an old friend of mine I'd like to show up," he said, and spit on the ground. "Mink. You know Mink? I told you, the guy I was in the army with. On account of what you said, I said for him to come around and take over this afternoon. The bastard owes me two bucks: I told him if he'd come around I'd forget it. So, baby," his reaching hand touched the cool silk of her blouse, "unless the guy shows up," and then, with a gentle pressure, slipped to her breast, "I guess I'm stuck here." They regarded each other silently for as long as it took a tear of sweat to slide from the top of his forehead down the length of his cheek. "I missed you," he said. And he would have said something more if a customer had not come rolling into the lot.

Three ladies from Westchester, in for lunch and a matinee; Grady sat in the car and waited while Clyde went to attend them. She liked the way he walked, the way his legs seemed to take their time, each step lazily spaced and oddly loping: it was the walk of a tall man. But Clyde was not much taller than herself. Around the parking lot he always wore a pair of summer khakis and a flannel shirt or an old sweater: it was a kind of dress better looking and far more suitable to him than the suit he was so proud of. He was usually wearing this suit, a double-breasted blue pin-stripe, whenever he appeared in her dreams; she could not imagine why; but for that matter, her dreams about him were unreasonable anyway. In them she was perpetually the spectator, and he was with someone else, some other girl, and they would walk past, smirking disdainfully or dismissing her by looking the other way: the humiliation was great, her jealousy greater, it was unreasonable; still, her anxiety had some basis: two or three times she was sure he had taken her car out driving, and once, after she had left the car there overnight, she had found lodged between the cushions a garish little compact, decidedly not her own. But she did not mention these things to Clyde; she kept the compact and never spoke of it.

"Ain't you Manzer's girl?" She had been dialing for music on the radio; she had not heard anyone approach, and so it was startling when she looked up and found a man leaning against the car, his eyes screwed on her and half his mouth crooked in a smile that showed a gold tooth and a silver one. "I said, you're Manzer's girl, huh? We saw the picture of you in the magazine. That was a good picture. My girl Winifred (Manzer tell you about Winifred?), she liked that picture a lot. You think the guy that took it would take one of her? It'd give her a big kick." Grady could only look at him;

and that, hardly: for he was like a fat quivering baby grown with freakish suddenness to the size of an ox: his eyes popped and his lips sagged. "I'm Mink," he said, and pulled out a cigarette which Grady allowed him to light: she began blowing the car-horn as loud as she could.

Clyde could never be hurried; after parking the Westchester car he ambled over at his own convenience. "What the hell's the racket?" he said.

"This man, well, he's here."

"So, you think I can't see that? Hiya, Mink." Turning away from her, he brought his attention to the floury smiling face of Mink, and Grady resumed her efforts with the radio: she was seldom quick to resent anything Clyde said: his tempers affected her only inasmuch as they made her feel closer to him, for that he released them against her so freely reflected the degree of their intimacy. She would have preferred, however, that nothing had been reflected in front of this ox-child: ain't you Manzer's girl? She had imagined Clyde talking of her to his friends, even showing them her picture in a magazine, that was all right, why not? On the other hand, her imaginings had not gone so far as to consider what sort of friends they might be. But it was pretty late in the day for climbing a high-horse; so, smiling, she tried to accept Mink, and said: "Clyde was afraid you might not be able to come. You're awfully nice to do this for us."

Mink beamed as if she had pressed inside him a light switch; it was painful, because she could see, by the new life in his face, that he knew she had not liked him and that it had mattered. "Oh yeah, yeah, I wouldn't let Manzer down. I'd have been here sooner, only Winifred, you know Winifred, she's on a strike from her job and she had me down there to tell off some big (pardon)." Grady's eyes fidgeted in the direction of the Nemo's little office-shack: Clyde had gone there to change his clothes, and she was anxious for him to come back, not only because being alone with Mink was nerve-racking but because, and it was as true of a minute ago as a week, she missed him. "That's a great car you got, sure is. Winifred's uncle, he's the one in Brooklyn, he buys used cars: bet he'd give you a load for that. Say, we all of us ought to double-date one night: drive out dancing, know what I mean?"

Clyde's reappearance relieved her of answering. Under a leather windbreaker he'd put on a clean white shirt and a tie; there was an attempt at a part in his hair and his shoes were shined. He planted himself before her, his eyes set apart and his hands cocked on his hips: the glare of the sun made him scowl, but his whole attitude seemed to say, how do I look? And Grady said, "Darling, you look just wonderful!"

Chapter 3

It had been her idea for them to lunch in Central Park at the cafeteria which adjoins the zoo. Because the McNeils' apartment was on Fifth Avenue and almost opposite the zoo, she had long since wearied of it, but today, goaded on by the novelty of eating out-of-doors, it seemed a gala notion; and furthermore, it would be all new to Clyde, for he drew a blank concerning certain sections of the city: the entire territory, for instance, that, beginning around the Plaza, stretches and widens up and eastward. This park-east world was naturally the New York Grady knew best: except for Broadway, she'd not often ventured out of it. And so she'd thought it was a joke when Clyde said he hadn't even known there was a zoo in Central Park; at least, that is, he had no memory of one. These ignorances intensified the overall riddle of his background; she knew the number and names of his family: there was a mother, two sisters who worked, a younger brother—the father, who had been a sergeant of police, was dead; and she knew generally where they lived: it was somewhere in Brooklyn, a house near the ocean that required over an hour by subway to reach. Then there were several friends whose names she'd heard often enough to remember: Mink, whom she'd just seen, another called Bubble, and a third named Gump; once she'd asked if they were real names, and Clyde had said sure.

But the picture she had devised from these oddments was too amateurish to deserve even the most modest frame: it lacked perspective and showed few talents for detail. The blame of course belonged to Clyde, who just was not much given to talk. Also, he seemed very little curious himself: Grady, alarmed sometimes by the meagerness of his inquiries and the indifference this might suggest, supplied him liberally with personal information; which isn't to say she always told the truth, how many people in love do? or can? but at least she permitted him enough truth to account more or less accurately for all the life she had lived away from him. It was her feeling, however, that he would as soon not hear her confessions: he seemed to want her to be as elusive, as secretive as he was himself. And yet she could not quite properly

accuse him of secretiveness: whatever she asked, he answered: still, it was like trying to peer through a Venetian
blind. (It was as if the world where they joined were a ship,
one becalmed between the two islands that were themselves:
with any effort he could see the shore of her, but his was lost
in the unlifting mist.) Once, armed with a far-fetched idea,
she had taken the subway to Brooklyn, thinking that if only
she could see the house where he lived and walk the streets
that he walked, then she would understand and know him as
she wanted to; but she had never been to Brooklyn before,
and the ghostly lonesome streets, the lowness of the land
stretching in a confusion of look-alike bungalows, of empty
lots and silent vacancy, was so terrifying that after twenty
steps she turned and fled down back into the subway. She realized afterwards that from the outset she'd known the trip
would be a failure. Perhaps Clyde, without conscious insight,
had chosen best in by-passing islands and settling for the soli-
tude of a ship: but their voyage seemed to have no port-of-
call of any kind; and, while they were sitting on the terrace of
the cafeteria in the shade of an umbrella, Grady had again
sudden cause to need the reassurance of land.

She had wanted it to be fun, a celebration in their own
honor; and it was: the seals conspired to amuse, the peanuts
were hot, the beer cold. But Clyde would not really relax. He

was solemn with the duties of an escort on such an excursion:
Peter Bell would have bought a balloon for mockery's sake:
Clyde presented her with one as part of a tenacious ritual. It
was so touching to Grady, and so silly, that for a while she
was ashamed to look at him. She held fast to the balloon all
through lunch, as if her own happiness bobbed and strained
at the string. But it was at the end of lunch that Clyde said:
"Look, you know I'd like to stay! Only something came up,
and I've got to be home early. It was something I'd forgot
about, or I would've told you before."

Grady was casual; but she chewed her lip before reply-
ing. "I'm sorry," she said, "that really is too bad." And then,
with a temper she could not detour: "Yes, I must say you
should've told me before. I wouldn't have bothered to plan
anything."

"What kind of things did you have in mind, kid?" Clyde
said this with a smile that exposed a slight lewdness: the
young man who laughed at seals and bought balloons had re-
versed his profile, and the new side, which showed a harsher
angle, was the one Grady was never able to defend herself
against: its brashness so attracted, so crippled her, she was left
desiring only to appease. "Never mind that," she said, forc-
ing a lewd note of her own. "There's nobody at the apartment now and I'd thought we'd go there and cook supper."

Tower-high and running halfway across a building, the windows of the apartment, as she had pointed out to him, could be seen from the cafeteria terrace. But any suggestion of visiting there appeared to upset him: he smoothed his hair and twisted tighter the knot of his tie.

"When do you have to go home? Not right away?"

He shook his head; then, telling her what she most wanted to know, which was why he had to go at all, he said: "It's my brother. The kid's having his bar mitzvah and it's only right I ought to be there."

"A bar mitzvah? I thought that was something Jewish."

Stillness like a blush came over his face. He did not even look when a brazen pigeon sedately plucked a crumb off the table.

"Well, it *is* something Jewish, isn't it?"

"I'm Jewish. My mother is," he said.

Grady sat silent, letting the surprise of his remark wrap round her like a vine; and it was then, while splashes of conversation at near tables rolled in waves, that she saw how far they were from any shore. It was unimportant that he was Jewish; this was the sort of thing Apple might have made an issue of, but it would have never occurred to Grady to consider it in any person, not Clyde certainly; still, the tone in which he'd told her presumed not only that she would, but emphasized further how little she knew him: instead of expanding, her picture of him contracted, and she felt she would have to start all over again. "Well," she began slowly. "And am I supposed to care? I really don't, you know."

"What the hell do you mean *care*? Who the hell do you think you are? Care about yourself. *I'm nothing to you.*"

An antique lady with a Siamese attached to a leash was listening to them rigidly. It was her presence that kept Grady in check. The balloon had wilted somewhat, the swell of it was beginning to pucker; still clutching it, she pushed back the table, hurried down the steps of the terrace and along a path. It was some minutes before Clyde could catch up with her; and by the time he did it was gone, the anger that had provoked and carried her away. But he held her by each arm, as if he supposed she might try to break loose. Flakes of sunlight falling through a tree lilted about like butterflies; at a bench beyond them a boy sat with a windup Victrola balanced on his lap and from the Victrola the eel-like song of a solo clarinet spiraled in the fluttered air. "You are something to me, Clyde; and more than that. But I can't discover it because we don't seem to be talking about the same things ever." She stopped then; the pressure of his eyes made language fraudulent, and whatever their purpose as lovers might be, Clyde alone seemed to understand it. "Sure, kid," he said, "anything you say."

And he bought her another balloon; the old one had

shriveled like an apple. This new balloon was far fancier; white and molded to the shape of a cat, it was painted with purple eyes and purple whiskers. Grady was delighted: "Let's go show it to the lions!"

The cat house of a zoo has an ornery smell, an air prowled by sleep, mangy with old breath and dead desires. Comedy in a doleful key is the blowsy she-lion reclining in her cell like a movie queen of silent fame; and a hulking ludicrous sight her mate presents winking at the audience as if he could use a pair of bifocals. Somehow the leopard does not suffer; nor the panther: their swagger makes distinct claims upon the pulse, for not even the indignities of confinement can belittle the danger of their Asian eyes, those gold and ginger flowers blooming with a bristling courage in the dusk of captivity. At feeding time a cat house turns into a thunderous jungle, for the attendant, passing with blood-dyed hands among the cages, is sometimes slow, and his wards, jealous of one who has been fed first, scream down the roof, rattle the steel with roars of longing.

A party of children, who had wedged themselves between Clyde and Grady, jogged and shrieked when the tumult began; but gradually, awed by the swelling tide of it, they grew quiet and clustered closer together. Grady tried to push through them; midway she lost her balloon, and a little girl, silent and evil-eyed, snatched it up and whisked herself off: both robber and robbery escaped almost unnoticed, for Grady, fevered by the lunging loin-deep animal sounds, wanted only to reach Clyde and, as a leaf folds before the wind or a flower bends beneath the leopard's foot, submit herself to the power of him. There was no need to speak, the tremble of her hand told everything: as, in its answering touch, did his.

In the McNeil apartment it was as if a vast snow had fallen, hushing the great formal rooms and shrouding the furniture in frosty drifts: velvet and needlework, the fine patinas and the perishable gilt, all were spook-white in their coverings against the grime of summer. Somewhere far-off in this gloom of snow and drawn draperies a telephone was ringing.

Grady heard it as she came in. First, before answering it, she led Clyde down a hall so sumptuous that if you at one end had spoken no one at the other would have heard: the door to her own room was the last on a line of many. It was the only room that the housekeeper, in closing the apartment, had left exactly as it was in winter. Originally it had belonged to Apple, but after her marriage Grady had inherited it. Much as she had tried to rid it of Apple's froufrou a good deal remained: nasty little perfume cabinets, a hassock big as a bed, a bed as big as a cloud. But she had wanted the room anyway, for it had French doors leading onto a balcony with a view over all the park.

Clyde lingered by the door; he had not wanted to come, had said he was not dressed right; and now the ringing telephone seemed to agitate further uncertainties. Grady made him sit down on the hassock. In the center of it there was a phonograph and a stack of records. Sometimes when she was alone she liked to sprawl there playing sluggish songs that nicely accompanied all kinds of queer thoughts. "Play the machine," she said, and, asking why in God's name it hadn't stopped, went to answer the phone. It was Peter Bell: dinner? Of course she remembered, but not there, and please, not the Plaza, and no, she didn't want Chinese food; and no, really, she was absolutely alone, what merriment? oh the phonograph—uh huh, Billie Holiday; all right, Pomme Souffle, seven sharp, see you. As Grady put down the receiver she made a wish that Clyde would ask who had called.

It was not to be granted. So, of her own accord, she said, "Isn't that lovely? I won't have to eat alone after all: Peter Bell's going to take me to dinner."

"Hmm." Clyde went on shuffling through the records. "Say, you got 'Red River Valley'?"

"I've never heard of it," she said briskly, and threw open the French doors. He at least could have asked who Peter Bell was. From the balcony she could see steeples and pennants far over the city quivering in a solution of solid afternoon: though even now the sky was growing fragile and soon would crumble into twilight. He might be gone before then; and thinking so, she turned back into the room, expectant, urgent.

He had moved from the hassock to the bed; sitting there on the edge of it, and the bed so big all around him, he looked wistfully small: and apprehensive, as though someone might walk in and catch him here where he had no business being. As if taking protection from her, he put his arms around Grady and rolled her down beside him. "We waited a long time for one of these," he said, "it ought to be good in a bed, honey." The bed was covered in blue and the blue spread before her like depthless sky; but it seemed all unfamiliar, a bed she could've sworn she'd never seen: strange lakes of light rippled the silk surface, the bolstered pillows were mountains of unexplored terrain. She'd never been afraid in the car or among the wooded places they'd found across the river and high upon the Palisades: but the bed, with its lakes and skies and mountains, seemed so impressive, so serious, that it frightened her.

"You cold or something?" he said. She strained against him; she wanted to pass clear through him: "It's a chill, it's nothing"; and then, pushing a little away: "Say you love me."

"I said it."

"No, oh no. You haven't. I was listening. And you never do."

"Well, give me time."

"Please."

He sat up and glanced at a clock across the room. It was after five. Then decisively he pulled off his windbreaker and began to unlace his shoes.

"Aren't you going to, Clyde?"

He grinned back at her. "Yeah, I'm going to."

"I don't mean that; and what's more, I don't like it: you sound as though you were talking to a whore."

"Come off it, honey. You didn't drag me up here to tell you about love."

"You disgust me," she said.

"Listen to her! She's sore."

A silence followed that circulated like an aggrieved bird. Clyde said, "You want to hit me, huh? I kind of like you when you're sore: that's the kind of girl you are," which made Grady light in his arms when he lifted and kissed her. "You still want me to say it?" Her head slumped on his shoulder. "Because I will," he said, fooling his fingers in her hair. "Take off your clothes—and I'll tell it to you good."

In her dressing-room there was a table with a three-way

mirror. Grady, unclasping a bracelet chain, could see at the mirror every movement of Clyde's in the other room. He undressed quickly, leaving his clothes wherever he happened to be; down to his shorts, he lighted a cigarette and stretched himself, the colors of sunset reflecting along his body; then, smiling toward her, he dropped his shorts and stood in the doorway: "You mean that? That I disgust you?" She shook her head slowly; and he said, "You bet you don't," while the mirror, jarred by the fall of her chair, shot through the dusk arrows of dazzle.

It was after twelve, and Peter, lifting his voice above the pulsing of a rumba band, ordered from the bartender another scotch; looking across the dance-floor, infinitesimal and so crowded the dancers were one anonymous bulge, he wondered if Grady was coming back. A half-hour before she had excused herself, presumably for the powder-room; it occurred to him now, however, that perhaps she'd gone home: but why? Simply because he hadn't applauded when she described, and evasively at that, the glories of romance? She should be grateful he hadn't told her a few of the things he had a mind to. She was in love; very well, he believed her, though that he must do so exasperated him: still, did she mean to marry whoever-it-was? As to this, he had not dared ask. The possibility she might was insupportable, and his reaction to it had so waked him that after these martinis and uncounted scotches, he felt still painfully sober. For the last five hours he'd known that he was in love with Grady McNeil himself.

It was curious to him that he had not before come to this conclusion from the evidence at hand. The cloud of sandcastles and friendship signed in blood had been allowed to obscure too much: even so, the evidence of something more intense had always been there, like sediment at the bottom of a cup: it was she, after all, with whom he compared every other girl, it was Grady who touched, amused, understood: over and again she had helped him to pass as a man. And more: part of her he felt was the result of his own tutoring, her elegance and her judgments of taste; the strength of will she so fervently possessed he took no credit for: that, he knew, was much the superior of his own, and indeed, it was her will that frightened him: there was a degree to which he could influence her, after that she would do precisely as she wanted. God knows, he had nothing to offer, not really. It was possible that he never could make love with her, and if he did probably it would dissolve into the laughter, or the tears, of children playing together: passion between them would be remarkable, even ludicrous, yes, he could see that (though he did not see it squarely): and for a moment he despised her.

But just then, sliding past the entrance rope, she beckoned to him, and he hastened to join her, thinking only, and with an awareness that seemed unique, how lovely she was, with what excellence she dominated over the flashing squadrons of important cockatoos. Her everyway hair was like a rusty chrysanthemum, petals of it loosely falling on her forehead, and her eyes, so startlingly set in her fine unpolished face, caught with wit and green aliveness all atmosphere. It was Peter who had told her she should not use makeup; it was also his advice that she looked best in black and white, for her own coloring was too distinct not to conflict with brighter patterns: and it gratified him that she was wearing a domino blouse and a tumbling long black skirt. The skirt swayed with the music as he followed her to a table; en route, his eyes discreetly totaled the amount of attention she received.

People did usually look at her, some because she suggested the engaging young person at a party to whom you would like to be introduced, and others because they knew she was Grady McNeil, the daughter of an important man. There were a few whose eyes she held for a different reason: and it was because, in her aura of willful and privileged enchantment, they sensed she was a girl to whom something was going to happen.

"Can you guess who I saw last week? At Locke-Ober's in Boston?" he said as soon as they were seated under the glare of a white cellophane tree. "You remember Locke-Ober's, McNeil? I took you to dinner there once, and you liked it because out in the alley there was a man with a banjo and a hat of brass bells. Anyway, I ran into an old friend of ours, Steve Bolton." It wasn't that he'd just remembered this encounter: rather, he'd selected to remember, intending it should recall for her the outcome of an old emotion which, regarded in retrospect, might give some doubt as to the merits of a current one: though what she may have once felt for Steve Bolton he merely suspected. "We had a drink together."

Grady said, "Steve: Lord, it's been years: or has it? No, I don't suppose it has. But whatever was he doing in Boston?" and this expressed accurately the quality of her interest. The thought that she'd loved him did not lean with embarrassing weight, as Peter assumed it would; besides, she'd never been ashamed of that. But she'd not thought of him in months, and he seemed as uncontemporary as the songs everyone had sung that summer.

"Up there on some sort of business, I should imagine. Or a class reunion: he's the type. I never liked him, you know, though I haven't much reason now: he looked pretty drained-out, and not quite so Steve-ish. He said if I saw you to give you his best."

"And Janet? How are Janet and the baby?"

Having discovered that Steve Bolton's name did not set off any commotion, Peter was bored with the subject. But Grady, waiting to hear, found her interest in Janet genuine: Janet, unlike Steve, was not seen at the small end of a telescope, but sharply in the foreground, present and punishing; and she remembered the morning when she'd prolonged Janet's agony (with a remorse never quite felt before). "Or didn't he mention them?"

"Yes, of course he did. Said they were fine. There's another one, a girl this time. You can be sure he showed me a picture: whatever makes people do that? All those glossy snapshots of gooey brats! Perverse. I hope you never have any children."

"Why, for God's sake? I'd like a little bowlegged baby: bathe it, you know, and hold it up in the light."

Here was a wedge and he used it. "A bowlegged baby? And what, my dear, would he think of that?"

"Who?" said Grady.

"You'll forgive me, I don't know the gentleman's name,"

he said, serving a point. "I'll venture to say, though, that it's one fairly well-known (come now, isn't this why you don't tell me?), that he is some sort of intellectual and at least twenty years older: nervous girls of extensive sensibility always get goose-happy over daddy-types."

Grady laughed, though laughter, she saw too late, authorized his making cartoons of her situation. She was willing to permit him this liberty, however: it was small payment for a service he'd done her this evening, one impossible to explain: it consisted simply in his now knowing Clyde Manzer existed; for his knowing it made Clyde dwindle to human size and exist, too. So long had she shrouded him in shadow and secret that he had come to loom greater than his actuality. To have another person know drained much of the mystery and lessened her fear of his dissolving: he was a substance at last, someone carried not just in her head, and mentally she floated toward him, ecstatic to embrace his reality.

Peter was pleased with himself. "You needn't bother answering: but am I right?"

"I won't tell you; if I did, then I shouldn't have any more of your theories."

"Do you want really to hear my theories?"

"No, as a matter of fact I don't," she said: as a matter of

fact, she did: it gave back something of the excitement of having still a secret.

"Tell me one thing." Peter speared his palm with a swizzle stick. "Are you going to marry him?"

She recognized the purposeful quality of his asking and, keyed to banter, was disconcerted by it. "I don't know," she said, with a resentful chop in her voice. "Does one always have to want to marry? I'm sure there are kinds of love in which that is hardly an issue."

"Yes: but aren't love and marriage notoriously synonymous in the minds of most women? Certainly very few men get the first without promising the second: love, that is—if it's just a matter of spreading her legs, almost any woman will do that for nothing. But seriously, dear?"

"Seriously, then (though obviously you're the one not being serious): I have no answer to give, how could I when I've never really thought of it? We came here to dance, darling. Shall we?"

Awaiting them on their return was a photographer, surly with disinterest, and the Bamboo Club's press agent, a sassy pouting man whose jeweled hands fluttered about the table arranging festive props: a champagne bucket, a vase of flowers, a monster-large ashtray on which the club's name was brazenly photogenic. "That's right, Miss McNeil, just a little picture, you don't mind? Now, now, mustn't stare at the camera, that's right, look at each other: *sweet,* absolutely darling, *couldn't* be cuter! Artie, you're taking a great picture, capturing young love, that's what you're doing. Ah, Miss McNeil, *I* know better—listen there, even your young man says I'm right! Don't you, young man? And who *are* you, anyway? Wait now, I want to write it all down. But isn't that someone awfully old or dead or famous or something, Walt Whitman? Oh, *I* see, you're Walt Whitman the second; a *grandson,* are you? Well, isn't that lovely. Thank you, Miss McNeil, and you, too, Mr. Whitman: you've both been *sweet,* absolutely darling." He did not forget to take with him the flowers, the champagne, the ashtray.

Peter's expense on whiskey had at last paid a dividend: which is to say, his sense of humor had reached a point that was without discrimination; and he was determined to push it even further: unfortunately, someone gave him an opportunity. It was a grey, inhibited little man who, goaded by his companion, a pink strawberry woman sipping brandy, leaned from the next table and gave Peter's arm a diffident peck: "Pardon me," he said, "but we wondered if you people are British royalty? My friend says because they took your picture you're British royalty."

"No," said Peter, with a patient smile. "American royalty."

Grady was persuaded they should leave: another minute and there would be a fight: it was with that expectation that Peter wanted to stay. He could at least be ashamed, he said, and got them as far as the dance-floor, but there he bogged down, insisting they dance and demanding the orchestra play his favorite tune: "Just One of Those Things." She warned him to stop singing in her ear: "Just one of those fabulous flights": so after a while she sang with him. A marathon of scarlet stars blinked on a circle of ceiling, and Grady, sprinkled by their light, dizzy in their whirl, drifted in the refuge of this sky: a voice, far down upon the earth, carried up to her: can you hear? that I say you are royalty? Dreaming, she thought it was Clyde, though how like Peter it sounded! And turning in space, her hair swung like a victory. They danced until all at once and as one the music dimmed and the stars went dark.

Chapter 4

"The doorman gave me these," said Clyde, almost a week later. He held out two telegrams, but Grady did not take them until she'd turned on the kitchen faucet and rinsed her hands of waffle-batter. "I'd like to take a poke at that guy: a real schnook! You ought to see the kind of looks he gives me. And that kid on the elevator, he's a little fairy: I'll hand him something to nibble on." She had heard these complaints before, they needed no comment from her, so she said: "Where's the butter, honey? And did you get the kind of syrup I wanted?" She was making a very late breakfast: they had not got up until after eleven. For the last few days the parking lot had been closed; the owner was having some trouble over his license. And the day before, accompanied by Mink and his girlfriend, they'd driven up into the

Catskills on a picnic. On the way back a tire had blown out, and it was two in the morning before they'd crossed the George Washington Bridge. "No soap on that syrup—so I got Log Cabin, O.K.?" he said, settling himself by the waffle-iron and unfolding a tabloid he'd brought back. His eyebrows, whenever he read, dipped like a scholar's (and with a mumbling noise he chewed one after another of his fingernails). "Says here Sunday was the hottest July sixth since 1900: over a million people at Coney—what do you think of that?" Grady, remembering the blazing rock-strewn field where they'd scrounged around battling insects and eating unsalted hard-boiled eggs, didn't think much. She finished drying her hands and sat down to open the telegrams.

Actually, one was a cable, an extravagant two-pager from Lucy in Paris: Safely here stop horrid voyage as daddy forgot dinner suit and we forced to stay evenings in cabin stop airmail dinner suit at once stop also send my hair switch stop put out the lights stop don't smoke in bed stop am seeing man tomorrow about your dress stop will send samples stop are you all right query tell Hermione Bensusan to mail me your horoscope for July and August stop am worried about you stop love mother. Grady creased the cable with a groan; did her mother really believe she was going to get her involved again with Hermione Bensusan? Miss Bensusan was an astrologist Lucy doted on.

"Hey, hurry up with those waffles. There's a ball-game on the radio."

"There's a radio in the cupboard," she said, not looking up from the peculiar message of her second telegram. "Turn it on if you want."

He touched her hand softly. "What's the matter: bad news?"

"Oh no," she said, laughing. "Just something rather silly." And she read aloud: "My nightly mirror says you are divine and the daily mirror says you are mine."

"Who sent it?"

"Walt Whitman the Second."

Clyde was fiddling with the radio. "Don't you know the guy?" he said, between scraps of broadcast.

"In a way."

"Must be a joker: or is he nuts?"

"A bit," she said, meaning it: once, during the time he was in the navy, and when his ship had touched at some Far East port, Peter had mailed her an opium pipe and fifteen silk kimonos. She had given all but one of the kimonos to a charity auction, a generosity that backfired when someone discovered the simple designs that patterned them were an illusionary trick: held in certain lights they revealed dreadful obscenities. Mr. McNeil, caught dead-center in the ensuing ruckus, had said, nonsense, obviously the value of the kimonos should increase: he hadn't objected at all to Grady's wearing one. In fact, she was wearing it now, though the cumbersome sleeves had a nasty habit of drooping into the bowl as she stood whipping up her waffle-batter.

She would not admit she was making a mess. Unfazed by bacon already shriveled and coffee stone-cold, she poured her mixings onto a grill she'd forgotten to grease, and said, "Oh I adore to cook: it makes me feel so mindless in a worthwhile way. And I've been thinking—if you're going to listen to a ball-game, why, I might bake a chocolate cake: would you like that?" Presently, with a gust of smoke, the waffle-iron indicated a charred content; twenty minutes later, having scraped the iron, she announced cheerfully, and not without pride: "Breakfast ready."

Clyde sat down and surveyed his plate with a smile so wan that she said, "What is it, darling? Couldn't you find your ball-game on the radio?" Hmm, he'd found the right station, but the game hadn't started yet: and would she mind heating up the coffee again? "Peter loathes baseball," she said, for no reason other than that it was a detail she'd just remembered: as an opposition to Clyde, who appeared so to guard his own talk, she'd begun saying whatever came into her head, regardless of how irrelevant. "Be careful," she said, carrying the percolator from the stove and pouring him more coffee, "you'll burn your tongue this time." As she passed he caught her hand, swinging it a little to and fro. "Thank you," she whispered. "Why?" he said. "Because I'm happy," she answered, and swung her hand free of his. "That's funny," he said, "it's funny you're not happy all the time," and his arm swept outward in a gesture she instantly regretted, for it indicated, indeed proved, how aware he was of her advantages: absurdly, she'd not thought him resentful.

"Happiness is relative," she said: it was the easiest reply.

"Relative to what: money?" This retort seemed to give his spirits a lift. He stretched, yawned, told her to light him a cigarette.

"After this, you'll light your own," she said, "because I'm going to be very busy with a chocolate cake. You can get some ice-cream from Schrafft's: won't that be heaven?" She propped a cookbook in front of her. "Lots of wonderful recipes in here: listen to this——"

Interrupting, he said, "It just came to me: did you mean that when you told Winifred she could have a party here? She's the kind of girl that'll think you meant it."

This derailed her own train of thought: what party? And

then, in a rainfall of memory that left her quite drenched, she remembered that Winifred was the dark, hefty, huge girl Mink had brought to the picnic in the Catskills: a picnic to which Winifred had contributed, in addition to a pound of salami, something near to two hundred pounds of giggling fat and muscle. Rhinoceros into wood-nymph, and clad in a pair of gym-bloomers, these a hold-over from athletic days at Lincoln High, she'd romped with nature all the afternoon, never letting go the clutch she kept on a sweaty bunch of daisies: there were some people who just thought it was funny the way she loved flowers, she said, but honestly there was nothing she loved better than flowers because that was the kind of person she was.

And yet, in an ill-defined way, she was admirable, Winifred. Like her spaniel eyes, there was a tender good kind of warmth in her unrestraint; and she so adored Mink, was so proud and solicitous of him. Grady knew no one she thought less attractive than Mink, or more preposterous than Winifred: yet together and around them they made a clear lovely light: it was as if, out of their ordinary stone, their massive unshaped selves, something precious had been set free, a figure musical and pure: she could not but pay it homage. Clyde, who, it would seem, had presented them as a warning that what was his would not suit her, appeared surprised that she liked them. But when the tire blew, and while the men were fixing it, Grady had been left alone in the car with Winifred; and Winifred, luring her into a cave of feminine confidence, quickly brought about one of the few times Grady had ever felt close to another girl. They each told a story. Winifred's was sad: she was a telephone operator, and that she liked, but her life at home was misery because, determined to marry Mink, she wanted to have an engagement party, and her family, who thought Mink worthless, would not allow it in the house: what oh what was she to do? Grady had said, well, if it was only a party, why she could use the McNeils' apartment. Promptly Winifred had burst into fat tears: it was the nicest thing, she said.

"Even if you did mean it," Clyde continued, "I don't think it's such a hot idea: if your family ever heard about it I'll bet there'd be hell to pay."

"Isn't it rather incongruous, your worrying about my family?" she said; and it flashed upon her that he was jealous; not of her, but of Mink and Winifred, for it was as if he believed she had bribed them away from him. "If you don't want the party, very well: I couldn't care less. I only offered to because I thought it would please you: after all, they're your friends, not mine."

"Look, kid—you know what it is between us. So don't go getting it mixed up with a whole lot of other things."

She smarted under this: it made her feel quite ugly; and, maintaining silence at a cost, she hid herself behind the cookbook. Most of all, she wanted to say to him that he was a coward: only a coward, she knew, would revert to such tactics; and she was tired, too, of the quiet he imposed upon her: he seemed so familiar with quiet, and to accept it so easily, that perhaps he did not understand guilt was something she herself, at least in relation to him, was far from feeling. Irritably, and with her recipe a blur on the page, she listened to the rustle of his paper. He was leaning back in a chair, and it came forward with a thud.

"Christ!" he said, "here's your picture," and twisted around so that she could see over his shoulder. A fuzzy, fly-specked image of her and Peter, both resembling embalmed frogs, stared from the paper. Clyde, following the print with his finger, read: "Grady McNeil, debutante daughter of financier Lamont McNeil, and her fiancé, Walt Whitman the Second, in private conversation at the Atrium Club. Whitman is a grandson of the famed poet."

It was outrageous, she could hear Apple telling her so: all the same, it took a stony comment from Clyde to stop her laughter: "Let somebody else in on the joke."

"Oh darling, it's so complicated," she said, wiping her eyes. "And anyway, it's nothing."

Tapping the picture, he said, "Isn't this the guy that sent the telegram?"

"Yes and no," she said, and despaired of explaining. But Clyde did not seem to care. With his eyes pinched and far-looking, he sucked in smoke and let it out slowly through his nose. "Is that true?" he asked. "Are you and what's-his-name engaged?"

"You know better than that: of course not. He's just an old friend, someone I've known all my life."

Scowling, he drew on the table a contemplative circle: his finger traced round and round it; and Grady, who had thought the subject ended, saw something more was to come. Her sense of this deepened as each circle evolved, evaporated; and the suspense brought her to her feet. She looked down at him, expectant. But it was as if he could not make up his mind what it was he had to say.

"Peter and I grew up together, and we—"

Clyde cleared his throat decisively. "I don't guess you know it, I guess maybe this is news: but I'm engaged."

The smallest affairs of the kitchen seemed suddenly to attack her attention: time passing in an invisible clock, the red vein of a thermometer, spider-light crawling in the Swiss curtains, a tear of water suspended and never falling from the faucet: these she wove into a wall: but it was too thin, too papery, and Clyde's voice could not be canceled. "I sent her a ring from Germany. If that's what engaged means. Well," he said, "I told you I was Jewish: or anyway my mother's—and she's crazy about Rebecca. I don't know, Rebecca's a nice girl: she wrote me every day I was in the army."

Distantly the telephone was ringing: Grady had never thought a call more important; ignoring the extension phone in the kitchen, she rushed through a maze of servant-halls into the outer apartment and her own room. It was Apple in East Hampton. Talk slower, Grady told her, for at the other end there was only a lot of words and sputter: trying to ruin the family? she said, when she realized that Apple's long-winded dramatics were related to Peter Bell and the newspaper picture: alas, someone had shown it to her. Ordinarily, she would have hung up; but now, when even the floor seemed unsubstantial, she held to the sound of her sister's voice. She wheedled, explained, accepted abuse. Gradually Apple softened to such a degree she put her little boy on the phone and made him say, hello, Aunt Grady, when you coming out to see us? And when Apple, taking up this theme, suggested she come and stay the week in East Hampton, Grady put up no struggle at all: before they hung up it was settled that she would drive out in the morning.

By her bed there was a cloth doll, a faded homely girl

with tangled strings of red raggedy hair; her name was Margaret, she was twelve years old, and probably older, for she'd not been much to look at when Grady had first found her forsaken by some other child and lying on a bench in the park. At home everyone had remarked how much alike they looked, both of them skinny and straggling and red-headed. She fluffed the doll's hair and straightened her skirt; it was like old times when Margaret had always been such a help: oh Margaret, she began, and stopped, struck still by the thought that Margaret's eyes were blue buttons and cold, that Margaret was not the same anymore.

Carefully she moved across the room and raised her eyes to a mirror: nor was Grady the same. She was not a child. It had been so ideal an excuse she somehow had persisted in a notion that she was: when, for instance, she'd said to Peter it had not occurred to her whether or not she might marry Clyde, that had been the truth, but only because she'd thought of it as a problem for a grown-up: marriages happened far ahead when life grey and earnest began, and her own life she was sure had not started; though now, seeing herself dark and pale in the mirror, she knew it had been going on a very long while.

A long while: and Clyde too much a part of it: she wished him dead. Like the Queen of Hearts, forever shouting off with their heads, it was all in her fancy, for Clyde had done nothing to warrant the severity of execution: that he should be engaged was not criminal, he was within his rights absolutely: for what in fact were her claims on him? There were none she could present; because, unadmitted but central in her feelings, she'd had always a premonition of briefness, a knowledge that he could not be sewn into the practical material of her future: indeed, it was because of this almost that she'd chosen to love him: he was to be, or was to have been, the yesteryear fire reflecting on snows soon enough to fall. Before she quit the mirror she'd seen that all weathers are unpredictable: the temperature was dropping, snows were already upon her.

She tipped back and forward on a seesaw of anger and self-pity. There was a limit to the charges to be brought against herself: she had a few in store for him. And chief among these was the compact she'd found in her car; with rather a flourish she extracted it from a bureau-drawer: hereafter, he could ride Rebecca on a trolley.

The hush and roar of baseball filled the kitchen; Clyde, biting his nails, was bending over the radio, but on her entrance his eyes cut anxiously sidewise. And she paused, wondering if really she should. In a moment, however, it was done: she had put the compact down beside him. "I thought

your friend might like to have this back: it must be hers—
I found it in the car."

A rush of shame smeared his neck; but then, after he'd
slipped the compact into his pocket, there was a steely top to
bottom hardening, and his husky voice went pit-deep:
"Thanks, Grady. She was looking for it."

It was as if an electric fan churned in Clyde's head, and the
drone of the sports announcer, caught in its whir, was a
sound clapped and crazy. He felt in his pocket for the compact and closed his hand on it hard: a snap, a tinkle, and it
burst: splinters of mirror pierced his palm, which bled a little.

He was sorry to have broken the compact, because it had
belonged to someone he'd loved, his sister Anne.

In April, when he'd first known Grady, a kink had devel-
oped in the fuselage channel of her Buick, an ailment he himself could not seem to remedy, and so he had taken the car
over to Brooklyn to show his friend Gump, who worked in a
garage. Anne used to hang around this garage most of the
day. A stunted, weazened girl of nineteen who looked no
more than ten or eleven, she'd understood motors as well as
a man. At home she'd collected a pile of scrapbooks high as
herself, and they contained nothing but the fantasia of her

own designs for super-speed automobiles and inter-planet aeroplanes. This had been her life's work, all she'd known, for when she was three years old she'd had a heart attack, and so had never gone to school. Despite a united effort in the family, no one had been able to teach her to read or write, she'd simply rejected every attempt, and gone defiantly on with her real concerns: the workings of an engine, the sweep of wings in outer space. There had been a rule in the house that one did not lift their voice to Anne: always, and by everyone except Clyde, she was given the ostentatious consideration shown someone expected to die: Clyde, who could not imagine that she would, who could not picture the house without her motor-talk and tool-tinkering, her fairy-tale wonder at the sound of a plane or the spectacle of a new car, had treated her with a natural robustness she'd answered by adoring him: we're brothers, aren't we, Clyde? was how she'd described her view of their closeness. And he was not ashamed of her. The others had been, somewhat. His sister Ida had been particularly disgruntled that Anne should be allowed to hang around all day in a garage: what do you suppose people think of me when there is my own sister dressed like a trollop and loafing with every bum in the neighborhood? Clyde had said truthfully that these boys Ida called bums were nuts about Anne: and they were the only friends she had. But it was more difficult to excuse the way she dressed. Until she was seventeen Anne had worn infantile clothes from Ohrbach's children's department; then, just one day, she bought herself a pair of three-inch heels, a razzle-dazzle dress or two, a pair of false breasts, a compact and a bottle of pearl-colored nail polish; swishing along the streets in her new décor, she looked like a little girl in masquerade: strangers laughed. Clyde had once beat up a man for laughing at her. And he'd told her never mind Ida and the rest: wear what she pleased. And she'd said, well, she didn't care personally what she wore, but that she wanted to look pretty because of Gump. Out of the clear sky she'd proposed to Gump, who had been nice enough to say that if he married anybody it would be Anne. It was because of this that Clyde counted him his best friend: he never complained when Gump cheated at cards. The day he had driven Grady's car out to the garage in Brooklyn, Anne was there: wearing high heels and with a rhinestone comb in her hair she was helping Gump locate a motor-knock. There was a spring rainbow in the sky, and the blending of a rainbow and a blue glittering convertible had been too much for her: in a car like that, she'd said, begging Clyde to take her for a ride, why, in a car like that you could reach the end of the rainbow before it faded away. So he had driven her all over the neighborhood,

and past a school where the children were letting out (even
the littlest ones know more than me, but they never were in
such a gorgeous car); perched sparrow-like on the top of a
seat, and dancing her legs, she'd waved to everyone, as
though she were the heroine of a big parade. And when he'd
stopped by their house to let her out, she'd thrown him a kiss
from the curb: he thought he'd never in all his life seen a
prettier girl. A few minutes later, hurrying up the stairs,
she'd plunged backwards and down: it was the Lord's mercy,
said Ida, who had been the only one at home, and who had
not reached her in time.

Clyde thought back: during those days when Ida and his
mother and Bernie and Crystal were collecting sympathy
and perpetuating funeral sorrow, he'd stayed away from
home and had a good time with Grady: you didn't want to
talk about Anne to a crazy kid like her. When he was in the
army he'd picked up a great many girls: sometimes nothing
happened except a lot of talk, and that was all right, too: because it didn't matter what you said to them, for in those tran-
sient moments lies or truth were arbitrary and you were
whatever you wanted to be. The morning he'd first seen
Grady at the parking lot, and later, when she'd been around
a few times and he'd known for sure there was something in
the air, she'd seemed to him like one of these girls, someone

on a train; and he'd thought what the hell: take what comes your way: so he'd asked her for a date. Afterwards, he did not understand her at all: she had in some way outdistanced him, overshot the mark of his expectations: a crazy kid, he said, knowing full well how inadequate a label this was, and yet, handicapped by the width of her feeling and the narrowness of his, he could not improvise another. It was only with retreat that he could keep the least position: the more important she became, the less he made her seem so: because, for Christ's sake, what was he supposed to do when she walked out? Which sooner or later she would. If he believed differently, then maybe he could share himself in the way she wanted, but the prospect facing him was all-subway and all-Rebecca, and to accept that meant he could not take too seriously a girl like Grady McNeil. It was hard. And becoming more so. At the picnic he'd gone to sleep for a while with his head on her lap; dreaming, someone had said it was not Anne who had died, but Grady: when he'd wakened, and seen her face in a halo of sunlight, there had been a breaking all through him: if he'd known how, it was then that he would have exposed the fraud of his indifference.

He emptied the broken compact out of his pocket into a waste can; whether or not Grady noticed he couldn't tell, for whenever he made a motion she averted her head, as if she were afraid their eyes might connect, or that he would touch her. Dazed, and moving with a clumsy stealth, she'd gathered the ingredients of a cake; but in separating her eggs she'd dropped a yolk into a bowl of whites, and she stood now staring at her mistake as though she'd reached an impasse not ever to be surmounted. Watching her, Clyde took pity: he wanted to go over and show her how easy it would be to lift out the yellow. But there was a huge roar from the radio; someone had hit a homer and he waited to hear who: again, though, he could make no sense of the game, and rather violently he turned the radio off. Baseball was a sore subject anyway, reminding him, as it did, of past achievements and promises unfulfilled and dreams gone up the flue. Long ago it had been a pretty settled thing that Clyde Manzer was going to be a champion ballplayer: everyone had praised him as the best pitcher in the sandlot league: once, after a no-hit game, and with the high-school band leading the way, he'd been carried from the field on a crowd of shoulders: he'd cried, and his mother had cried too, though her tears had been motivated by more than pride: she'd been sure Clyde was ruined, and that now he would never live up to her plan of his being a lawyer. It was funny how it had all fallen through. Not a single talent scout approached him; no college offered a scholarship. He'd played a little ball in the army, but there no one had noticed him particularly; nowadays he had to be cajoled into a game of catch, and for him the lonesomest sound in all Brooklyn was the crack of a ball on a bat. Launching about for another career, he decided he wanted to be a test-pilot; and so after joining the army he'd applied for air-corps training: insufficient education was the reason they'd given for rejecting him. Poor Anne. She'd sat Ida down and dictated a letter: *Let them jump in a lake, precious brother. They are boobs. It is you who will be the first to fly one of my space ships. And someday we will set foot on the moon.* Ida had added a practical postscript: *Better you should think about Uncle Al.* Uncle Al ran a small luggage factory in Akron; more than once he'd offered to take his brother's son into the business—a proposition that offended Clyde, the baseball champion: however, following his army discharge, and after a few upside-down midnight months of sleeping all day and running around all night, he'd one morning found himself on a bus to Akron, a city he hated before he'd half got there. But then, he hated most places that were not New York; away from it over any period and he dried up with misery: to be elsewhere seemed a waste of time, an exile from the main current into sluggish by-streams where life was flat and spurious. Actually, Akron had not been so dull. He'd liked his job, if only because it had carried some authority—

four men worked under him: yessir, son, Uncle Al said, we're going to turn us a buck together. All this might have worked out had it not been for Berenice. Berenice was Uncle Al's only child, an overdeveloped spoiled pussycat with mad milk-blue eyes and a tendency toward hysteria. There was nothing innocent about her; from the start it was clear that she knew a thing or two, and no more than a week passed before she made decided overtures. He was living at Uncle Al's house, and one night at dinner he felt her foot under the table; she'd removed her shoe, and her warm silken foot, rubbing along his leg, so aroused him he could not hold a fork steady. It was an incident he afterwards considered with the greatest shame: to be excited by a child seemed unnatural and frightening. He tried to move to a Y.M.C.A. in downtown Akron, but Uncle Al wouldn't hear of it: we like you around the house, boy—why, just the other night Berenice was saying how much happier she is since her cousin Clyde came to live here. Then one day, while he was drying himself after a shower, he caught the pale blue of an unmistakable eye shining through the bathroom keyhole. Every fury inside him boiled to the surface. Wrapped in a towel, he flung open the door; and Berenice, backing blindly into a corner, had stood mute and hangdog while he heaped on her a vast dirt of army swear-words: too late he realized that, from the top of the stairs, Uncle Al's wife had heard everything. Why do you talk that way to a child? she'd asked quietly. Not taking the time to answer, he'd put on his clothes, packed and walked out of the house. Two days later he was back in New York. Ida said what a pity it was he hadn't liked the luggage business any better.

Restless ants of energy, scrambling in his muscles, stung him into a need for action. He was fed up: with himself, and with Grady's pensive brooding, which depressed him in much the same way as did the long-sorrow sessions at which his mother was so capable. As an adolescent he'd had a compulsion to steal, for the dangers involved had been his most effective way of retaliating against boredom; in the army, and for rather similar reasons, he'd once stolen an electric razor. He felt an impulse to do something of the sort now. "Let's get the hell out of here," he exploded; then, more quietly: "There's a Bob Hope picture at Loews." With a fork Grady speared the misplaced egg yolk. "We might as well," she said.

It was wilting out on Lexington Avenue, and especially so since they'd just left an air-conditioned theater; with every step heat's stale breath yawned in their faces. Starless nightfall sky had closed down like a coffin lid, and the avenue, with its newsstands of disaster and flickering fly-buzz sounds of neon, seemed an elongated, stagnant corpse. The pavement was wet with a rain of electric color; passersby, stained by these humid glares, changed color with chameleon alacrity: Grady's lips turned green, then purple. Murder! Their faces hidden behind tabloid masks, a group, steaming under a streetlamp and waiting for a bus, gazed into the printed eyes of a youthful killer. Clyde bought a paper, too.

Grady had never spent a summer in New York, and so had never known a night like this. Hot weather opens the skull of a city, exposing its white brain, and its heart of nerves, which sizzle like the wires inside a lightbulb. And there exudes a sour extra-human smell that makes the very stone seem flesh-alive, webbed and pulsing. It wasn't that Grady was unfamiliar with the kind of accelerated desperation a city can conjure, for on Broadway she'd seen all the elements of it. Only there it was something she'd known vicariously, and she had not, as it were, taken part. But now for her there was nowhere an exit: she was a member.

She stopped to straighten her socks, which had crawled down into her shoes; and she decided then to wait a moment, wondering how long it would take Clyde to realize he'd left her behind. On the corner was an open-air store, and the sidewalk there was like an amazing garden where fountains are fruit and the flowers are arranged in bunches of large parasols. Clyde stood an instant there, then walked rapidly back to meet her. And she wanted to hurry him through the streets, hide with him in the dark of the apartment. But: "Go across the street," he said, "and wait for me in front of that drugstore."

A curious tension thinned his face; because of it, she did not ask him why he wanted her to wait there. Her view of him was confined to glimpses grabbed between bursts of traffic; presently she caught sight of him revolving around the fruit and flower store. It was at this moment, too, that she recognized coming toward her a girl who had been in her class at Miss Risdale's: so she turned and, looking into the blazing windows of the drugstore, studied a display of athletic supporters. A roar from underground echoed through her, for she was standing on top of a subway grating: deep in the hollows below she could hear a screeching of iron wheels, and then, nearer by, there came a fiercer noise: car-horns clashed, fenders bumped, tires careened! and she whirled around to see a driver cursing at Clyde, who was jayhopping across the street as fast as his legs would go.

Snatching her hand, he pulled her along with him, and they ran until they reached a side street muffled and sweet with trees. As they leaned together, panting, he put into her hand a bunch of violets, and she knew, quite as though she'd seen it done, that they were stolen. Summer that is shade and moss traced itself in the veins of the violet leaves, and she crushed their coolness against her cheek.

When she got home she called Apple to say she would not be coming to East Hampton after all. Instead, she drove with Clyde to Red Bank, New Jersey, and they were married there around two o'clock in the morning.

Chapter 5

Clyde's mother was an ample, olive-dark woman with the worn and disappointed look of someone who has spent her life doing things for others: occasionally the mulling plaintiveness of her voice suggested that she regretted this. "*Kinder, kinder,* I'm asking, a little control," she said, touching fingertips to her forehead; her hair, ribbed like a washboard and riveted by tiny combs tight against her head, rippled with silver zigzags. "Bernie darling, do like Ida says, don't bounce balls in the house. Go for Mama into the kitchen and help your brother with the icebox."

"Don't push!"

"Push him?" said Ida, who had done the pushing. "I'll cripple the little dope. I'm telling you, Bernie, you bounce balls in the house and I'll cripple you."

To which Mrs. Manzer reiterated her first plea. Her ears

were pierced with jet, and these beads tossed like bells as she waved her head, sighing an indistinguishable epithet. On a table beside her there was a small potted cactus-plant, and she tamped the earth around it; Grady, who was sitting opposite, remarked that it was the ninth or tenth time she had repeated this gesture, and deduced that Mrs. Manzer was quite as uneasy as herself: a deduction which helped her to relax somewhat.

"You understand, my dear lady? Oh I see, you smile and nod your head; but it is impossible: you have no brothers in your family."

Grady said, "No, as a matter of fact I have just one sister," and reached in her purse for a cigarette; but, as there were no ashtrays around, she doubted that smoking would be acceptable to Mrs. Manzer, and so withdrew her hand, wondering, alas, what to do with it: all the parts of herself seemed so cumbersome, which was a good deal Ida's fault, for Ida, during the last hours, had subjected her to a scrutiny fine as lacework.

"A sister only? That is a shame. But you will have sons I hope. A woman without sons has no consequence: she is not well thought of."

"Well, count me out," said Ida, a stark, vindictive girl with kinky hair and a sallow, sullen expression. "Boys are hateful; men, too. The fewer the better, I say."

"You talk foolish, Ida dear," said her mother, removing

the cactus-plant to a window-shelf, where a square of Brooklyn sunlight fell upon it desolately. "That is a dried up way of talking; you want more juice in you, Ida dear. Maybe you better go to that mountain place like Minnie's girl did last year."

"She wasn't to any mountain. Believe me, I've got the news on her."

It was uncommon, the extent to which Mrs. Manzer and her older son duplicated each other's traits and features: that blurred ambiguous half-smile, those imposing eyes, the slow spacing of words that characterized the speech of both: it was heart-quickening for Grady to see these characteristics reproduced, and to see them employed to so different an effect. "The man is everything, a delicate everything," she said, disregarding her daughter's insinuation, which also was very like Clyde, who ignored whatever he chose to. "And the man inside the child: that is what a mama must guard and trust, like Bernie: a sweet boy, so good to his mama, an angel. That was my Clyde, too. An angel. If he had a Milky Way he always gave his mama half. I'm very fond of Milky Ways. But now; yes, boys grow up changed and they don't remember the mama so well."

"See? Now you're saying the same thing I say: men are ungrateful."

"Ida, dear, please, do I complain? It is right a child should not love the mama the way the mama loves the child; children are ashamed of the love a mama has for them: that is part of it. But when a boy grows into a man it is right his time should be for other ladies."

A quiet settled upon them, and there was nothing strained about it, as there often is when silence falls among new acquaintances. Grady thought of her own mother, of the complicated affections that had passed between them, the moments of love that—out of disbelief? unforgiving doubt?—she had rejected; and considering what chance there was of making these up, she saw there was none, for only a child could have done so, and the child, like the chance itself, was gone.

"Ah, what is worse than an old woman who talks too much, a *yenta?*" said Mrs. Manzer with a lively sigh. She was looking at Grady: it was not a look that asked, why did my son marry you? for she didn't know they were married; but: why does my son love this girl? is for any mother a deeper question, and Grady could read it in her eyes. "You are polite and listen. But I will hold my tongue now, and listen to you."

In imagining the visit to Brooklyn, Grady had conceived of herself as an invisible witness wandering unobserved into the parts of Clyde's life that took an hour to reach by subway: only at the door had she realized how unrealistic this was, and that she, as much as anyone else, would be on view: who are you? what have you to say? It was not presumptuous that Mrs. Manzer should ask, and Grady, meeting the challenge, forced herself forward: "I was thinking—I'm sure you're wrong—about Clyde," she stammered, having seized the nearest subject. "Clyde is so terribly devoted to you."

She knew at once that she had spoken out of turn, and Ida, with a look just this side of haughty, lost no time in telling her so: "All Mama's children are devoted to her; she has had a lot of good fortune in that respect."

An outsider so indiscreet as to comment on the loyalties of a family must expect reprimand, and Grady accepted Ida's with a grace that implied she did not know it was one. For indeed the Manzers were a family: the used fragrance and worn possessions of their house reeked of a life in common and a unity no fracas could disrupt. It belonged to them, this life, these rooms; and they belonged to each other, and Clyde was more theirs than he knew. For Grady, who, in this sense, had little sense of family, it was a strange, a warm, an almost exotic atmosphere. It was not, however, an atmosphere she would have chosen for herself—the airless inescapable pressures of intimacy with others would have withered her soon enough—her system required the cold, exclusive climate of the individual. She was not afraid to say: I am rich, money is the island I stand on; for she assessed properly the value of this island, was aware its soil contained her roots; and because of money she could afford always to substitute: houses, furniture, people. If the Manzers understood life differently, it was because they were not educated to these benefits: their compensation was in a greater attachment to what they did have, and doubtlessly for them the rhythm of life and death beat on a smaller but more concentrated drum. It was two ways of being, at least that is how she saw it. Still, when all is said, somewhere one must belong: even the soaring falcon returns to its master's wrist.

Mrs. Manzer smiled at her; quietly, with the persuasive, firelight voice of a storyteller, she said: "When I was a girl I lived in a little city on the side of a mountain. There was snow on top and a green river at the bottom: can you see it? Now listen, and tell me if you can hear the bells. A dozen towers, and always ringing."

Grady said, "Yes, I do," and she did; and Ida, impatient, said, "Is this about the birds, Mama?"

"Strangers who came there called it a city of birds. How true. Of an evening, when it was almost dark, they flew in clouds, and sometimes it was not possible to see the moon rise: never have there been so many birds. But in winter it was bad, mornings so cold we could not break the ice to wash our faces. And on those mornings you would see a sad thing: sheets of feathers where the birds had fallen frozen: believe me. It was my father's job to sweep them up, like old leaves; then they were put into a fire. But a few he would bring home. Mama, all of us, we nursed them until they were strong and could fly away. They would fly away just when we loved them most. Oh, like children! Do you see? Then when winter came again, and we saw the frozen birds, we always knew in our hearts that here and there was one we'd saved from some winter before." The last bright ash in her voice guttered and darkened; musing, withdrawn, she took a low, shuddering breath: "Just when we loved them most. How true."

And then she touched Grady's hand, saying: "Can I ask, what's your age?"

It was as if the fingers of a hypnotist had popped close to her eyes: alerted, turned out of a slumber where the cherished, slain by other winters, burned in wing-fluttering fires, she blinked and said, "Eighteen"; no, not yet, it was weeks ahead, her birthday, almost two months of days uncut, not tarnished, like a cherry pie or flowers, which suddenly she wanted to claim: "Seventeen, really. I won't be eighteen until October."

"Seventeen, I am already married; eighteen, I am the mother of Ida. That is the way it should be: young people married young. A man will work then." She spoke vehemently; and with more color than seemed necessary: this, fading rapidly, left her pensive. "Clyde will be married. I have no worry."

Ida giggled. "If you don't, Clyde does—have worries, I mean. I saw Becky in the A&P this morning, and she was just furious; so I said, what's eating you, honey? And she said, Ida, you can tell that brother of yours to go sit on a tack."

It was as though Grady were abruptly transferred to a harsh and damaging altitude; with a ringing in her ears, she waited, not knowing by what path to descend.

"Rebecca is angry?" said Mrs. Manzer, the merest seed of concern planted in her tone. "Why is that now, Ida?"

She lifted her shoulders: "I should know? What do I know that goes on between those two? Anyway, I said she should come around today."

"Ida."

"So why do you say Ida, Mama? There's plenty enough for everybody to eat."

"Jesus, you're just going to have to get a new icebox: nobody could fix that one anymore." It was Clyde, who, having approached unnoticed, stood at the edge of the room, smeared top to bottom with grease and holding a frayed Frigidaire belt. "And look, Ma—can't you make Crystal step on it: you know I've got to be back to work at four." Right behind him, Crystal appeared with a rushing defense of herself: "I'm asking you, Mama, what do you think I am? a horse? an octopus? All day I've been in that kitchen while you people loll in the cool parts of the house—and Bernie sent in there to drive me wild, and Clyde with the icebox all over the floor." Mrs. Manzer held up her hand, which brought everyone's grievances to a halt; she did know how to handle them. "Hush now, Crystal darling. I'll come in there and do it myself. Clyde, clean yourself; and Ida, you go set the table."

Clyde lingered after the others: dim, at a distance, a statue; his shirt was silk-wet with sweat and pasted to him like a thin plating of marble. Long ago, in April it was, Grady had taken of him a mental photograph, an intense, physical picture, emphatic as a cut-out on white paper: alone, often isolated by midnight, she let it emerge, an intoxicating symbol that set her blood to whispering; now, as he came closer, she closed her eyes, and retreated toward the beloved image, for her husband, looming above her, seemed a distortion, another person.

"You all right?" he said.

"Why shouldn't I be?"

"Yeah?" He slapped his thigh with the Frigidaire belt. "Well, remember, it was you that wanted to come."

"Clyde. I've thought it over. And I think we'd better tell them."

"I can't do that. Aw, honey, you know damn well I can't, not yet."

"But Clyde, but something, I—"

"Take it easy, kid."

For minutes, like a circulating presence, the sour sweet sweat smell of him stayed in the air, but a trifling breeze passed through the room, taking him with it: so she opened her eyes, lonely. She stopped by a window and rested on a cold radiator. Screeching roller-skates rubbed the street like chalk squealing on blackboard; a brown sedan cruised by, its radio loudly playing the national anthem; two girls carrying bathing suits tripped along the sidewalk. Inside, the Manzers' house was much the same as it was outside, where, divided from the sidewalk by a runt-sized hedge, it was one in a block of fifteen houses, which, while not exactly alike, were still more or less indistinguishable assemblages of prickly stucco and very red brick. Similarly, Mrs. Manzer's furniture had this look of anonymous adequacy: chairs enough, plenty of lamps, a few too many objects. It was, however, only the objects that reflected a theme: two Buddhas, splitting their sides, supported a library of three volumes; on the mantel, tipsy jug-toting Irishmen laughingly jigged; an Indian maiden, made of pink wax, carried on a dreamy smiling ceaseless flirtation with Mickey Mouse, whose doll-sized self grinned atop the radio; and, like comic angels, a bevy of cloth clowns gazed down from the tall heights of a shelf. Such was the house, the street, the room: and Mrs. Manzer had lived between a green river and a mountain's white summit in a city of birds.

Trilling his tongue, and with a model aeroplane suspended above him, Bernie scooted into the room. He was a whiny, worm-white, unwilling child, with banged-up bandaged knees, a baldy haircut and daredevil eyes. "Ida said I should come talk to you," he said, whizzing around like a bat out of hell; and Grady thought, yes, Ida would. "She dropped Ma's best plate and it didn't break but Ma's mad anyway on account of Crystal's burnt the meat and Clyde's let the icebox flood." He collapsed and squirmed on the floor as though someone was tickling him. "Only why is she mad about Becky?"

Grady, feeling slightly unethical, smoothed her shirt and, surrendering to impulse, said: "I wouldn't know; is she?"

"I hope to tell you; and it just seems funny to me, that's

all." He flipped the propeller of his aeroplane, then said: "Ida said Crystal dared her, and that just seems funny 'cause Becky comes here all the time without nobody daring her. If it was all my house, I'd tell her to stay home. She don't like me."

"What a beautiful little plane! Did you build it yourself?" Grady said suddenly, for there were footsteps in the hall which made her anxious. Actually she did admire the plane, it was unusual; its fragile skeleton and stretchings of delicate paper were joined with Oriental care.

He pointed proudly to an imitation leather frame in which several Kodak pictures were placed together. "You see her? She made it. That's Anne. She made thousands and millions, all kinds."

The gnomish, spook-like little girl, whom Grady assumed to be a playmate of his, held her attention not an instant, for, to the left of this child, there was a picture of Clyde, smartly turned out in an army uniform and with his arm slung cozily around the waist of an indistinct but vaguely pretty girl. The girl, wearing a skirt much too short and a corsage far too large, was holding an American flag. As she looked at the picture, Grady felt a chill echo, the kind that comes when, in an original situation, one has the sensation of its all having occurred before: if we know the past, and live the present, is it possible that we dream the future? For it was in a dream that she'd seen them, Clyde and the girl, running arm in arm, while she, on an escalator of voiceless protest, slipped past and away. It was to happen, then; she would suffer in the daytime; and thinking so, she heard Ida's voice, which fell like a long crashing tree: pinioned by its weight, she cringed in her chair. "I took all these myself, just nuts about taking pictures: aren't they cute? That one of Clyde! It was right after he was in the army, and they had him down in North Carolina, so Becky got me to go down on the train with her, a lot of laughs! And that's where I met Phil. He's the one in the bathing suit. I don't see him anymore; but the first year he was out of the army we were engaged and he took me dancing thirty-six times, the Diamond Horseshoe and everywhere like that." There was a history attached to each picture, and Ida recounted them all, while in the background Bernie played cowboy songs on an ancient phonograph.

What infinite energies are wasted steeling oneself against crisis that seldom comes: the strength to move mountains; and yet it is perhaps this very waste, this torturous wait for things that never happen, which prepares the way and allows one to accept with sinister serenity the beast at last in view: resignedly Grady heard the doorbell ring, a sound that, when it came, jabbed into the composures of everyone else (except Clyde, who was upstairs washing his hands) like a hypodermic needle. Though she had at this moment every reason to walk out, she was determined not to make a poor show, and so when Ida said, "Here she is now," Grady only looked toward the host of angel clowns, surreptitiously poking her tongue at them.

Chapter 6

The next day, Monday, marked the start of a memorable heat-
wave. Although the morning papers said simply fair and
warm, it was apparent by noon that something exceptional
was happening, and office-workers, drifting back from lunch
with the dazed desperate expression of children being bul-
lied, began to dial Weather. Toward midafternoon, as the
heat closed in like a hand over a murder victim's mouth, the
city thrashed and twisted but, with its outcry muffled, its
hurry hampered, its ambitions hindered, it was like a dry
fountain, some useless monument, and so sank into a coma.
The steaming willow-limp stretches of Central Park were
like a battlefield where many have fallen: rows of exhausted
casualties lay crumpled in the dead-still shade, while newspaper photographers, documenting the disaster, moved sepul-

chrally among them. In the cat house at the zoo, the suffering lions roared.

Aimlessly Grady moved from room to room, where at many angles clocks winked maliciously, all dead, two proclaiming twelve, another three, one saying a quarter to ten; out of mind, like these clocks, time flowed in her veins— thick as honey, each moment refusing to be used up: on and on, like the prowling golden cryings of the lions, which, fading at the windows, she heard but dimly, a sound she could not identify. Nostalgic, gingery hints of Spanish geranium wafted in her mother's room, and Lucy, diamond-studded, an ermine stole crushed around crinkling evening glitter, swept spectrally past, her artificial party voice reaching back: go to sleep, my darling, sweet dreams, my darling; and the after-scent of Spanish geranium said laughter, fame, said New York, winter.

She waited on the threshold. The green sublime room was in appalling disarray: its summer coverings were stripped back, a spilled ashtray sprawled on the silver rug, there were crumbs and cigarette ashes in the bed, which was unmade: mixed in among the sheets was one of Clyde's shirts, and a pair of his shorts, and a lovely old fan that belonged to a set Lucy had collected. Clyde, who stayed over in the apartment three and four nights a week, liked the room, and had taken it for his own; he kept his extra clothes in Lucy's private closet, so that his khaki trousers always smelled faintly of Spanish geranium. But Grady, as if she didn't understand why it should have this invaded, burglarized look, cussed the room with an aghast expression; she could only think: something ruthless has happened here, so heartless I shall never be forgiven; and she finicked about, attempting to straighten up, and she picked up his shirt, then stood there, stroking her cheek with the sleeve of it.

He loved her, he loved her, and until he'd loved her she had never minded being alone, she'd liked too much to be alone. At school, where all the girls had crushes on one another and trailed in sweetheart pairs, she had kept to herself: except once, and that was when she'd allowed Naomi to adore her. Naomi, scholarly, and bourgeois as a napkin ring, had written her passionate poems that really rhymed, and once she'd let Naomi kiss her on the lips. But she had not loved her: it is very seldom that a person loves anyone they cannot in some way envy: she could not envy any girl, only men: and so Naomi became mislaid in her thoughts, then lost, like an old letter, one which had never been carefully read. She had liked to be alone, but not, as Lucy accused, to spend her time in listless moping, which is a vice of the highly domesticated, the naturally tame: there pumped through her a nervous wild vigor that every day demanded steeper feats, more daring exertions: the police warned Mr. McNeil about her driving; twice she was caught on the Merritt Parkway making eighty and over. It wasn't a lie when she told the arresting officers that she'd had no idea how fast she was going: speed numbed her, turned out the lights in her mind, most of all it deadened a little the excess of feeling that made personal contacts so painful. Others struck the keys too hard, and too loud were the chords she played back. Think of Steve Bolton. And Clyde, too. But he loved her. He loved her. If the telephone would ring. Perhaps it will if I don't look at it; it does that sometimes. Or was he in terrible trouble, was that why it never rang? Poor Mrs. Manzer, weeping, and Ida, shouting, and Clyde: go home, I'll call you later, those were his exact words, and how long could she endure it, alone among stopped clocks and heat-hushed sounds that faded at the windows? She sank on the bed, her blue-flooded head slipping sleepily downward.

"Christ, McNeil, doesn't the bell work? I've been standing here a half-hour."

"I'm asleep," she said, peering at Peter with sleep-sullen, disappointed eyes. She wavered at the door: suppose Clyde should come while Peter was here? All things considered, it was no time for them to meet.

"You needn't stare at me as though I was a nightmare," he said, amiably pushing past her. "Though I must say I feel like one—having spent this filthy day on a day-coach, and surrounded by little hoodlums, all just bursting with energy after their two weeks of fresh air. I hope you don't mind if I use your shower?"

She did not want Peter to see into the plunder of her mother's room, and so she hurried along the hall ahead of him. "I remember: you've been on Nantucket," she said as they went into her room, where immediately he unbuttoned a sticky seersucker jacket. "I got your card."

"Oh, did I send you one? That was thoughtful of me. As a matter of fact, we wanted you to come; I called a thousand times but no answer. We went up on Freddy Cruikshank's sailboat, and it was really rather fun, except that I got bitten by a crab—in a place I can't show you: speaking of which, turn around, I want to take off my pants."

Sitting with her back to him, she lighted a cigarette. "It must have been fun," she said, recalling other years, seaside summers white with sails, starfish, reverse summers. "I haven't been out of town since I saw you."

"Which is fairly apparent, wouldn't you say? You look like a lily: a little funereal for my taste." He was bragging: his own neat, very cared-for body was a color like tea, and sun streaks whipped through his hair. "I thought you were a devotee of the great outdoors; or did that belong to your tomboy days?"

"I haven't been feeling awfully well," she said, and Peter, already in the bathroom, paused to ask if it were anything serious. "Not really, no. The heat, I suppose. I'm never ill, you know that." Only yesterday. It was after Brooklyn; she remembered crossing the bridge, then stopping for a traffic light. "Only yesterday, I fainted," and as she said it something inside her turned over, fell down: a sensation not unlike what she'd felt when the traffic light had started to spiral and darkness happened. It had lasted a moment, the light, in fact, had scarcely changed; even so, there had been a blasting of car horns: sorry, she'd said, jumping her car forward.

"Can't hear you, McNeil. Speak up."

"It doesn't matter. I was just talking to myself."

"That, too? You are in a bad way. We both need some sort of soothing, a martini or two. Can you remember not to use sweet vermouth? I've told you so often, but it doesn't seem to do any good."

Glistening, altogether revived, he came out of the bathroom, and found an arrangement: a shaker of satisfactory martinis, on the phonograph "Fun to Be Fooled," at the glass doors sunset fireworks and a postcard view. "I can't enjoy this for long," he said, falling among the hassock cushions. "It's stupid, but I'm having dinner with someone who may give me a job: in radio, of all things," and so they made a toast that wished him luck. "It isn't necessary, I'm lucky anyway, wait, by the time I'm thirty I will have had the worst kind of success, be able, organized, someone who laughs at people that want to lie under a tree," which was not a frivolous prophecy, as Peter, sipping his drink, wisely knew, knowing, too, that it probably was the happiest thing that could happen to him, for the man described he secretly, irrevocably admired. And the lady with a flower garden, this was Grady, the wife worthy of pearls for Christmas, who entertains at an impeccable table, whose civilized presence recommends the man, that is what she seemed in his expectations, and, watching her pour him another cocktail, just as she might some dusk five years hence, he thought of how the summer had gone, not seeing her once, never calling, all days dragging toward the day that, having exhausted herself with whoever he was, she would turn to him, saying Peter, is it you? And yes. Passing him his drink, Grady noticed with dismay an unwarranted apprehension in Peter's eyes, a greediness about the mouth very foreign to the exuberant plan of his face; as their fingers touched around the glass stem, she had a sudden preposterous notion: is it possible, are you in love with me? And this skimmed like a gull, which presently she shooed out of sight, it was such a silly creature, but it came back, kept coming back, and she was forced to consider what Peter meant to her: she wanted his goodwill, she respected his criticisms, his opinions mattered, and it was because they did that she sat now half-listening for Clyde, more than dreading that he should arrive, for Peter, passing judgment, would make her reckon with what she'd done, and she had no heart for it, not yet. They let the room darken, and the surface of their voices, soft, yielding, stirred and sighed around them, what they talked of seeming not to matter, it was so much enough that they could use the same words, apply the same values, and Grady said, "How long have you known me, Peter?"

Peter said, "Since you made me cry; it was a birthday party, and you dumped a mess of ice-cream and cake all over my sailor suit. Oh, you were a very mean child."

"And am I so different now? Do you think you see me as I really am?"

"No," he said, laughing, "for that matter, I wouldn't want to."

"Because you might not like me?"

"If I claimed to see you as you really are, it simply would mean that I dismiss you, that I think you shallow and a bore."

"You could think much worse of me."

Peter's silhouette moved against the deepening green doors, his smile flickered, like the lights across the park, for, feeling her dishonesty, a sense of ghostly struggle had seized him: it was as if they were two figures pummeling around in wrapped sheets: she wants to excuse herself from blame without confessing why it is I might have cause to blame her. "Much worse than being a bore?" he said, jacking up his smile. "In that case, you were right to wish me luck."

He left soon afterwards, leaving her alone in the dark room, illuminated time to time by shocking leaps of heat-lightning, and she thought, now it will rain, and it never did, and she thought, now he will come, and he never did. She lighted cigarettes, letting them die between her lips, and the hours, thorned, crucifying, waited with her, and listened, as she listened: but he was not coming. It was past midnight when she called downstairs and asked the door-man to have her car brought around. Lightning jumped from cloud to cloud, a sinisterly soundless messenger, and the car, like a fallen bolt, streaked through the outskirts of the city, through humdrum night-dead villages: at sunrise she glimpsed the sea.

Leave me the hell alone, he told Ida when she came hunt-ing him out at the parking lot, and Ida said: you're a fine one, aren't you? Hit your own mama, and there she is in bed with a broken heart, not to mention Becky, and she says her brother says he'll kill you, so listen, I'm just warning you, that's all. But he hadn't hit his mama, Ida was only saying that to make it worse; or had he? He'd gone blind there a minute, seeing those tricksters in the hall, and oh how he'd fixed them: this is my wife, he'd said, and after the way they'd carried on, by Jesus if he'd ever set foot in that house again. As if he didn't know why they held on to him; sure, an extra paycheck was a good thing to have around: love, had they loved Anne? except he was sorry if he'd hit his mama, please God, he hoped he hadn't hit his mama. All his boyhood he'd stolen Baby Ruths and taken them to her; and Milky Ways that they put in the icebox and cut into little slices: my Clyde is an angel, he buys his mama candy bars. My Clyde will be a famous lawyer. Did she think he liked working in a parking lot? That he was doing it just to spite her, when all the time he could be a famous lawyer, a famous anything? Things happen, Mama. And Grady McNeil was part of the things that happen. But what of Grady? She'd walked out the door, and that was the last time he'd seen her. Bubble said: lay off that phone, save your nickels, she's just sore. Only she hadn't been sore, so it didn't make sense, unless it was because he hadn't shown up that night: well, so he had gone to the bar where Bubble worked and had one hel-luva time: sometimes you got to be by yourself, right? And if she was going to stay married to him, then they'd have to find a new way of living. For one thing, he wanted her to get out of that apartment. He knew a house on Twenty-eighth Street where they could get a couple of rooms. Now where was she? Aw, sit still, said Bubble. Bubble was over thirty, he worked as a bartender in an out-of-the-way nightclub; he was a friend from army days, and he was like his name, round, bald, thin-skinned.

One morning, it was the fourth day of the heat wave, Clyde woke up and felt an arm around him; he thought he was waking up with Grady, and his heart began to kick: honey, he said, snuggling deeper, gee baby, I missed you. Bubble let out a big snore, and Clyde pushed him away. He was living in Bubble's place, a furnished room far uptown; there was a Chinese laundry downstairs, in the street summer-wilted children were always crying chink! chink! and some mornings there was an organ-grinder, he was there now, his penny tunes clinking like the coins housewives tossed to the pavement. He missed her, colored balloons, flower wagons reminded him of that, and he rolled to the far side of the bed; he lay there, nursing an image of her, and with a gliding hand he stroked his parts. Cut it out, said Bubble, leave a guy get his sleep, and Clyde moved his hand away, ashamed, but Grady remained, wavering, unfulfilled, and he remembered another girl, one he'd seen in Germany: it was a spring day, clear, cloudless, he was walking in the country and, crossing a bridge that spanned a narrow crystal river, he looked down and saw, as though they were riding below the surface, two white horses attached to a wagon, their reins twisted around the arms of a young girl, whose drowned broken face glimmered under the dancing water; he took off his clothes, thinking he would cut her loose, but he was afraid, and there she remained, wavering, unfulfilled, beyond him in death as Grady seemed in life.

He gathered his clothes on tiptoe, then crept out the door; there was a pay-phone in the hall, he dialed her number, as usual no one answered. A swarm of kids buzzed around him on the stoop downstairs, hey, mister, give me a cigarette, and he barged through them, swinging his elbows, and one smart aleck, a skinny girl in a moth-eaten bathing suit, said hey, mister, button up your fly, and she ran after him, pointing. Jesus, he said, and grabbed her by the shoulders: her hair flared, floated, her face, pasty with terror, seemed to undulate, like the face of the girl in the river, to blur, as Grady's did when he tried to see her hard, whole, as his own, and his hands went limp, he ran across the street, the kids hollering: pick on somebody your own size. And who would that be, somebody his own size, when he felt so small and mean?

Seating himself at the counter of a White Castle, he ordered orange juice; it was too hot for anything else, not that he minded the heat, for in weather like this, New York, disowned by half its population, seemed to belong as much to him as to anyone else. While waiting for the orange juice, he rolled back his sleeve cuff and examined a stinging fresh tattoo that circled his wrist like a bracelet. It had happened the night before, banging around town with Gump; Gump and his damn reefers, let him smoke a stick or two and he always came up with some crazy idea, such as: I know a character will give us a swell tattoo for free. Gump knew some characters all right, this one lived in a coldwater flat in Paradise Alley, and he lived alone except for six Siamese and a stuffed python called Mabel: oh my dear boys, you should've known your old mother in those days, when Mabel was alive! What mad camps we were, so jolly, such fun, everyone adored us, several kings and all the queens ha ha, yes, we played the world together, dancing, dancing, twelve weeks in London alone, Waldo and Sinistra, Sinistra, that was Mabel's stage name, poor darling, she'd be alive this very minute if it wasn't for those filthy airlines, it really is too sick-making;

you see, they wouldn't allow Mabel on the plane, this was in Tangier and we'd had an imperative call to Madrid, so I simply wrapped her around me and put on an overcoat; everything was fine until somewhere over Spain she began to squeeze, I know how she felt, poor smothering baby, but it was absolute agony, Mabel getting tighter and tighter until finally I simply fainted, whereupon they hacked her in half with a knife, said it was the only way they could get me loose, those butchers! Ah, well—a flag, a flower, your sweetheart's name? This isn't going to hurt a bit. But it had hurt; G-R-A-D-Y, the letters of her name, blue and red and linked with a line, were still afire, so he bought a bottle of baby oil, and sat on an open-top Fifth Avenue bus massaging it into his wrist. He got off the bus near the Frick museum; walking park-side and under the trees, he started downtown, his eyes darting over the diamond-squared stones, an old habit that meant he was searching for lost valuables, money: twice he'd found rings, once a twenty-dollar bill, and today he stooped to pick up a nickel; straightening, he looked across the street, and he was where he wanted to be, opposite the McNeils' apartment house.

Look at Mr. Fat Ass: the doorman, swallow-coated, cotton-gloved, who does the bastard think he is, puffing like a pigeon? Ah, no sir, Miss McNeil is not at home, ah, no sir,

I'm afraid she left no message. But he could not face the doorman down; he could only spit behind the bastard's back. He crossed the street again, and paced up and down under the trees, hitching his shoulders. Then he saw little Leslie, the elevator boy, a cherub with pink cheeks and a sugary mouth; he came darting under the trees: hey there, he said, love furtively filling his eyes, look, I know where she is, only don't tell *him* I told you, and he said the doorman had been forwarding mail to Miss McNeil at her sister's house in East Hampton. He seemed hurt when Clyde offered him a half-dollar. So what d'ya want me to do, kiss you? said Clyde, and little Leslie, retreating, said fiercely: who d'ya think you're kidding?

He'd thought he would go crazy, there alone on the glaring acre of scorched gravel, and the afternoon like a greasy bubble that would never burst; but Gump showed up with a handful of real Havana cigars and a bottle of gin. Gump was on vacation, and they sat in the parking-lot shack enjoying the treats he'd brought and playing two-handed stud. Clyde couldn't keep his mind on the game, he lost twenty-two consecutive deals, so he threw down his cards and leaned in the doorway, sulking; late-day shadows surged, swayed, he saw night coming toward him, and he said, listen, you want to make a little trip with me? Because he was afraid to go alone.

. . .

All this would go on, these waves, these sea roses shedding sun-dried petals on the sand; if I die, all this will go on: and she resented that it should. She raised up among the dunes and drew a scarf across her thighs, then let it slide down again, for there was no one to see that she was naked. It was a coarse, unprofessional beach, crudely vast and scattered with old bones of driftwood. Grand people, preferring the club's beach, never used it, though some, like Apple and her husband, had built houses along the line. Every morning after breakfast Grady packed a box lunch and stayed hiding among the dunes until the sun kneeled sea-level and the sand grew cold. Sometimes she stood by the water, letting foam rinse around her ankles. She'd not ever distrusted water, but now each time she wanted to plunge out between the waves, she imagined them concealing teeth, tentacles. Just as she could not advance into the water, so she could not cross the threshold of a crowded room: Apple had given up asking her to meet anyone; twice they'd quarreled over this, once especially when Grady got all dressed for a dance at the Maidstone Club, then changed her mind and refused to go: and Apple said, I just think you'd better see a doctor, don't you? Grady could have answered that she had: Dr. Angus Bell, a cousin of Peter's who practiced in Southampton. Afterwards, she felt she'd known the truth longer than was possible—considering that she was not quite six weeks pregnant. In the house she'd found a medical book, and at night, locking the guest room door, she studied the portraits of lurid, fist-tight embryos, the lace-like veins, veil-like skin and coagulating eyes, which, curled as in sleep, hung to the roots of her heart. When? at what moment? the afternoon it rained? she was sure it had happened then, it had been so much the best: lying there, safe from the cool shadowy rain, and Clyde kicking back the covers to join her with a gentleness more gentle than the closing of an eyelid. If I died (in Greenwich she'd heard so often about Liza Ash, the much loved Liza who knew the words of every song: and Liza Ash had bled to death in a subway toilet) all this will go on. Shells in the tide, ships far off and going farther.

Or drawing nearer. According to a letter just received by Apple, her mother and *your poor father* were sailing from Cherbourg the sixteenth of September, which meant they would be home in less than a month: *Tell Grady please to have Mrs. Ferry come in from the country as she is sure to have made a mess—God knows I should have left Mrs. Ferry in charge—as we are not up to another mess having just seen what those Germans left of the house in Cannes simply unbelievable and an-*

other thing tell Grady her dress has turned out more marvelous
than a dream simply unbelievable.

At last there arrives a time when one asks, what have I
done? and for her it had come that morning at breakfast
when Apple, reading the letter aloud, reached this mention of
the dress; forgetting she'd not wanted it, and knowing only
that now she never would wear it, she fled down the stairs of
a new and mysterious grief: what have I done? The sea asked
the same, keen gulls repeated the sea. Most of life is so dull it
is not worth discussing, and it is dull at all ages. When we
change our brand of cigarette, move to a new neighborhood,
subscribe to a different newspaper, fall in and out of love, we
are protesting in ways both frivolous and deep against the
not to be diluted dullness of day-to-day living. Unfortunately, one mirror is as treacherous as another, reflecting at
some point in every adventure the same vain unsatisfied face,
and so when she asks what have I done? she means really
what am I doing? as one usually does.

The sun was weakening, and she remembered that
Apple's little boy was having a birthday party for which oh
god she'd promised to organize games. She slipped on her
bathing suit and was about to step onto the open beach
when she saw two horses cantering through the shallow
surf. Astride the horses were a young man and a handsome

girl with black streaming hair; Grady knew them, she'd played tennis with them the summer before, but now she couldn't recall their name, P-something and part of the younger manic set: rather charming, especially the wife. Up the beach they rode, their voices uniting in thrilled hoopla, and back they stormed, the drenched horses glistening like glass. Dismounting not far from where she lay hidden, and leaving their horses to cavort, they clambered over the dunes and fell with lovely laughter into a cove of high grass; it was quiet then, gulls glided soundless, sea breeze shivered the grass, and Grady thought of them curled there together, protected by a world that wished them well. Malice prompted her to show herself. Rising, she walked directly past them, and her shadow, skimming over them like a wing, was meant to shatter their pleasure. In this it failed, for the P-somethings, made innocent by the world's goodwill, could not feel a shadow. She ran down the beach, inspired by their victory, for through them she felt she'd seen the future as it bearably could be, and as she climbed the stairs leading from beach to house she unexpectedly found herself looking forward to children and a birthday.

At the top of the stairs she met Apple, who it appeared had been on the point of descending. The encounter surprised them, and they stepped far apart, regarding each other rudely. Grady said, "How's the party going? Sorry if I'm late." But Apple, rescrewing an earring with a petty precision that seemed to suggest their meeting had jarred it loose, looked at her as if she could not place her, as if, in fact, they needed to be introduced. It had the double effect of putting Grady on guard and off. "Really, I'm sorry if I'm late. Just let me run up and slip on a dress."

Apple stalled her, saying, "You haven't seen Toadie on the beach?" Toadie: an excruciating nickname for her husband, George. "He went out looking for you."

"He must've gone a different way. But isn't it a little silly, his going to look for me? I promised I'd be back to help with the party."

Apple said, "You needn't bother about the party," and a disturbing tremor twitched the corners of her mouth. "I've sent the children home; Johnny-baby's crying his heart out."

"That can't very well be my fault," Grady said, uncertain, waiting. "I mean: why are you frightening me?"

"Am I? I should've thought it the other way round, which is to say: why are you frightening me?"

"Oh?"

Then Apple made herself clear; she said: "Who is Clyde Manzer?"

A flag lily, pulled from a stalk next to the path, tore apart in Grady's hands, its colored scraps scattering like discarded theater stubs. It was such a long time before she said, "Why do you want to know?"

"Because not more than twenty minutes ago I was told that he was your husband."

"Who told you that?"

She merely said, "He did," but her pretty little face had gone suddenly wretched. "He came out from town in a taxi-cab; there was another boy with him, and Nettie let them in, I suppose she thought they had something to do with the party—"

"And you saw him," said Grady softly.

"He asked for you, the short one, and I said, are you a friend of my sister's? because actually it didn't seem to me that you could know him; and then he said, no, we're not friends, but I'm her husband." There was an intermission, a sound of waves rocked the silence, and then, while both avoided the other's eyes by gazing at the pieces of broken flag lily, she asked if this were true.

"That we're not friends? I suppose so."

"Please, dear, I'm not angry, really I'm not, but you must tell me: what have you done?"

What have you done what have I done, like an echo in a cave that reduces all to nonsense. She would so much rather someone had a tantrum, it was the sort of thing she'd prepared for. "But you are an idiot," she said, summoning an amazingly natural laugh. "This is one of Peter's tasteless jokes; Clyde Manzer is a friend of his from college."

"I would be an idiot if I believed you," said Apple, sounding like her mother. "Do you think I would ruin Johnny-baby's birthday over a joke? Of course that boy is no college friend of Peter's."

Lighting a cigarette, Grady sat down on a rock. "Of course he isn't. As a matter of fact, Peter's never seen him. He works in a parking lot, and I met him there last April; we were married not quite two months ago."

Apple moved a little up the path. She seemed not to have heard, though presently she said, "No one knows this, do they?" She watched Grady shake her head. "Then there isn't any reason why anyone should. Naturally it can't be legal, you aren't eighteen, twenty-one, whatever it is. I'm sure George will agree that it isn't legal; the thing to do is keep our heads, he'll know perfectly what can be done." Her husband waved at them from the beach, and she hurried to the stairs, calling his name.

Beyond him Grady saw the horses: dashing their hooves in the surf, splendid as horses in a circus; and remembering the promises they signified she caught Apple's wrist: "Don't tell him! Only that it's a joke of Peter's. Oh listen to me, I've got to have these next weeks, please, Apple, give them to me." They held to each other, balancing, and Apple whispered, "Stop it," as if her voice were lost. "Take your hand off me." But when Grady tried to release her, she discovered that really it was Apple holding on to her, and she twisted in this embrace, smothering with a sense of the scene gathering in upon her: the horses charged forward, George was on the stairs, Clyde she felt not far away. "Apple, I promise you, three weeks." Apple turned away from her, and went toward the house: "He's waiting for you at the Windmill," she said, not looking back. A mist had risen on the water, and the horses, scarcely seen, streaked by like birds.

A waitress, her apron appliquéd with chintz windmills, put two beers on the table and lighted a lamp. "You gentlemen staying for dinner?" Gump, who sat cutting his nails with a pocketknife, spit a piece of nail toward her: "So what have you got?"

"To start with, we have got Cape Cod oysters or shrimp New Orleans style or New England clam chowder—"

"Bring us the chowder," said Clyde, just to shut her up. It was fine for Gump, he'd had a good time thumbing comic books and fooling with girls on the sluggardly Long Island local that had brought them out; but Clyde had sat the whole way as though he were riding a roller coaster. Once when the train stopped a butterfly had lazied through the open window; he'd caught it in a peppermint sack, and the sack sat before him on the table: it was a present for Grady.

A bell jangled as she closed the door, and she saw Clyde's face, leaner, less sturdy, flash in the light; someone she'd never seen shook her hand, Gump, a lanky boy with stained skin wearing a summer shirt gaudy with shimmying hula dancers, and she felt the stubble of Clyde's unshaven chin against her cheek. "I know. I know," she said, avoiding his reconciling whisper. "It isn't anything to talk about now; not here."

"Say, who's going to pay for this?" cried the waitress, wagging bowls of chowder, and Gump, following out after Clyde and Grady, said: "Send me a bill, honey."

They all three fitted into the front seat of Grady's car. Clyde drove, and she sat in the middle. Her unrelaxing profile discouraged talk, and they drove in silence; winding round curves, the car left a trail of tension. It was not that she meant to be cold; rather, she meant nothing, felt little, except, perhaps, a fallen-in, ironed-out apathy. An orange moon was mounting like an airship, and road signs, studded with glass that leapt before their lights like cat eyes, said NEW YORK 98 MILES, 85.

"Sleepy?" said Clyde.

"Oh so sleepy," she said.

"Got just the thing." Gump spilled the contents of an envelope into his hand, a dozen or so cigarette ends. "Only roaches, but they'll wake us up."

"Go on, Gump, put that stuff away."

Gump said, "To hell with you," and lighted a butt; "Look," he said to Grady, "here's how you do it": he swallowed the smoke as though it were something to eat; "Have a drag?" Like a drowsy patient who never questions what the nurse brings she took the cigarette and kept it until Clyde jerked it away; she thought he was going to toss it out; instead, he smoked it himself. "You've got the idea—get your jumps from Doctor Gump." The butts were passed again, one for each, and someone turned on the radio: *You are listening to a program of recorded music.* Ash sparks darted, and their faces grew smooth as the young moon. *Let's take a kayak to Quincy or Nyack, / Let's get away from it all.* "Feel good?" said Gump, and she told him that she didn't feel anything, but a giggle escaped her, and he said, "You're doing fine, honey, just keep it up." It was Clyde saying, "I forgot your present, it was a present I brought you, a butterfly in a candy sack," that set her off: like fish-bubbles the giggles rose and burst into laughter, and, laughing, she slung her head from side to side—"Don't! Don't! It's too funny." No one knew quite what was funny, yet they all were convulsed; Clyde, for instance, could hardly hold the car to the road. A boy on a bicycle, careening before the rush of their head-lights, plunged into a fence. But even if they had killed the boy the laughter could not have stopped: it was all so hilari-ous. A scarf loosened off Grady's neck and trickled into the dark; and Gump, producing his envelope, said, "Let's pick up again."

A red votive haze hung over New York, but as they streaked across the Queensboro Bridge, the city, seen sud-denly full-length, went off like a Roman candle, each tower a crumbling firework of speeding color, and "I want to dance!" cried Grady, applauding the voluptuous skyline. "Throw off my shoes and dance!" The Paper Doll is a flimsy side-street catchall somewhere in the East Thirties, and Clyde took them there because it was the club where Bubble tended bar. Bubble, who saw them come in, coasted up, hiss-ing: "You crazy? Get her out of here. She's stoned." But Grady had no intention of leaving, she welcomed the sleep-less neon, the wiseguy faces, and Clyde had to follow her onto the dance floor, which was too small and knockabout for dancing: they simply held on to each other.

"All these days. I thought you were running out on me," he said.

"You don't run out on people; you run out on yourself," she said. "But it's all right now?"

"Sure," he said, "it's all right now," and danced her a cautious step or two. It was a curious trio that played for them: a silken Chinese youth (piano), a colored woman who peered respectably through steel schoolmarm spectacles (drums), and another Negro, a tall, especially black girl whose sleek splendid head shivered in the green pallor of an overhead light (guitar). There was no difference between tunes, for their music sounded all the same, jellied, jazzy, submerged.

"You don't want to dance anymore," Clyde said, as the trio rounded out a set.

"Yes, yes; I'm not going home," but she let him lead her over to the corner where Gump had got them a table.

The guitarist joined them. "I'm India Brown," she said, holding her hand out to Grady. It was a hand that felt like an expensive glove, but the fingers were thick and long as bananas. "Bubble says I should take you to powder your nose."

Grady said, "Bubble bubble bubble."

The colored girl leaned on the table; her eyes were like cuttings of dark quartz, and they filmed over, dismissing Grady; in a thin conspiratorial voice, she said, "It's none of my business what you boys are up to. But see that fat man

toward the end of the bar? Got this place spotted—just waiting for the chance to slap on a padlock. One little noise from
chicken like *her* and we're out. Sincerely."

Noise? Singsong lurched in Grady's head, and her eyes
halted on the fat man: he regarded her over the rim of a beer
glass. Standing next to him there was a tanned young man in
a trim seersucker suit, who, carrying a drink, sidled across
the room. "Get your things, McNeil," he said, seeming to
speak down from vast heights. "It's time somebody took you
home."

"Look, my friend, let's get this straight," said Clyde,
partly rising.

"It's only Peter," said Grady; like so much that was happening, his being there didn't strike her as unreasonable, and
she recognized him as though she were immune to surprise.
"Peter, darling, sit down; meet my friends, smile at me."

Simply, Peter said, "You'd better let me take you home,"
and lifted her purse off the table. A waiter, bringing a tray of
drinks, pulled back, and Bubble, his mouth a galvanized O,
bent over the bar: the distant crash of a passing elevated vi-
brated the tinseled room. Clyde walked around the table: it
was not a fair match, for, though Peter was taller, there was
no muscle to him, nothing of Clyde's scrappiness; and yet
Peter met a measuring appraisal with ready-and-willing

glances of his own. Clyde's hand shot out fast as a snake's thrust; he snatched back the purse and put it down beside Grady, who, just then, saw his exposed wrist: "You've hurt yourself," she said in a hardly alive voice, and touched the raw tattooed letters of her name; "for me," she said, raising her eyes, first to Clyde, whom she could not see, and then to Peter, whose white, intolerably stern face seemed to whittle away. "Peter," she said strangely, and sighing, "Clyde has hurt himself. For me." Only the Negro girl moved; she put her arm around Grady, and together, weaving a little, they went to the ladies' room.

As long as I am here, nothing can happen to me, she thought, letting her head loll against the guitarist's hard breasts. "He brought me a butterfly," she said, talking into a brown and peeling mirror. "It was in a peppermint sack." The guitarist said, "There's a way to the street: through that door, then out the kitchen," but Grady smilingly replied, "I thought it was a peppermint, it tasted just as sweet: feel my head, feel it flying?" To have her head held was pacifying, it lulled the sway there, the power-dive sound: "And sometimes it flies in other parts of me, my throat, my heart." The door opened, and the little drummer, looking like a rather lewd schoolteacher, came in brassily snapping her fingers. "All clear," she trumpeted. "Hooper gave those sonsabitches the bounce, and not a broken head so far. No fault of yours," she added, turning on Grady. "You hop-heads give me a fucking pain, always messing round." But the guitarist, gently smoothing Grady's hair with her banana fingers, said, "Oh shove it, Emma—she don't know what it's all about." The little drummer looked long at Grady: "Know what it's all about, sugar? I'll say!"

At the curb a sailor stood urinating; except for him, there was no one on the street, a brownstone street where they had parked the car; and yet the car was not there, so Grady circled under a lamp, soberly considering possibilities: that the car had been stolen, or: what? Funnel pipes, part of some street-construction project, spit gloomy gushers of steam, and the sailor, wreathed in these outpourings, seesawed over the pavement. She fled down to Third Avenue, where the slowly swinging headlights of a car struck her starkly.

"Hey, you!" shouted the driver, and she blinked: it was her own car with Gump at the wheel. "Sure it's her," he said; then she heard Clyde: "Hurry it up, put her in there with you."

Clyde was in the backseat, and Peter Bell was there, too; together, each straining against the other, they seemed a solid, double-headed, tentacled creature: Peter, his arm jacked behind his back, was hunched over, and his face, wrinkled like tinfoil, and bleeding, so shocked Grady that something gave way: she screamed, and it was as if for months this scream had been accumulating, but there was no one to hear her, neither in the stony emptiness of spinning streets, nor in the car: Gump, Clyde, even Peter, they were bound together by dumb deaf rapture—there was joy in the stupefying smash of Clyde's fists, and as the car screeched up Third Avenue, dodging El pillars, oblivious to red lights, she stared silently, like a bird that has stunned itself dashing against walls and glass.

For when panic emerges, the mind catches like the rip cord of a parachute: one goes on falling. Turning right on Fifty-ninth, the car skidded onto the Queensboro Bridge; there, above the hollow hootings of river traffic, and with a morning he was never to see changing the sky, Gump cried, "Damn it, you'll kill us," but he could not loosen her hands from the steering wheel: she said, "I know."

Afterword

To Truman I was, almost from the first, the "avvocato"—his lawyer. But I was also his friend. When I first met him in 1969 he had many friends, both famous and infamous. He was hands down the greatest gossip of his day and people flocked to him. By the time he died in 1984, at Joanne Carson's house in Los Angeles shortly before his sixtieth birthday, he had few friends left, having allowed his wit to turn poisonous and his imagination to distort reality almost beyond recognition. Over the years I tried to rescue him from many ill-advised and sometimes downright scary relationships, at times more successfully than others. Over these same years, particularly near the end, I had the sad, often heartbreaking, task of placing him in various drug and alcohol rehabilitation centers from which he invariably escaped, often with a highly amusing and improbable tale to tell.

The last time I saw Truman alive was at a restaurant opposite his apartment at United Nations Plaza in New York, where we often met for lunch. As was his custom then, he arrived early and the waiter put before him what he claimed was a large glass of orange juice but what the waiter and I both knew was a glass half filled with vodka. And it was not his first. I had asked rather urgently for our meeting because the doctor who treated him when he had passed out in Southampton, Long Island, had called and told me that unless he stopped drinking he would be dead in six months and that in fact his brain had shrunk. I reported this directly and pleaded with Truman to get back into rehabilitation and stop drinking and taking drugs if he wanted to survive. Truman looked up at me and there were tears in his eyes. He put his hand on my arm, looked straight into my eyes and said, "Please, Alan, let me go. I want to go." He had run out of options and we both knew it. There was nothing more to be said.

Truman never wanted to make a will. As with many people, he found it uncomfortable to contemplate. However, as his health deteriorated I succeeded in making him realize that he had to do something to protect his work after he died. Finally, he agreed to a very short and simple will, which, after providing for his great friend and former lover Jack Dunphy, left everything including his literary properties to a trust of which he insisted I be the sole trustee. His instruction was that I arrange for an annual award for literary criticism in memory of his good friend Newton Arvin. When I asked what we should do with the rest of the money, he said he doubted there would ever be any, but if there was I should provide scholarships in creative writing at universities and colleges of my choosing. In vain I asked for more specific instructions. He left me with the very Truman-like assurance that he was positive I would know just what to do and would do it better than he could.

Since his death, and with the invaluable support of my wife, Louise, I have tried to do what he would have wanted, and now there are Capote scholarships in universities such as Stanford, Iowa, Xavier, and Appalachian State, all dedicated to the hopeful emergence of bright new Capotes, all with their own unique voice and energy.

Since Truman's death, as trustee of The Truman Capote Literary Trust, I have made many decisions regarding the publication and other exploitation of his works in various media throughout the world. Until the resurrection of *Summer Crossing* in late 2004, my most difficult decision had been whether or not to publish in book form the three chapters of what was to be Truman's next major novel, *Answered Prayers*. Among his other great talents, Truman was a great dissembler and it was often very difficult to tell whether he was reciting fact or fiction. As his health and abilities deteriorated he dissembled more and more, particularly when it came to his writing output. As a result of the huge success of *In Cold Blood* I was able to make very advantageous contracts with his publisher, Random House, for the publication of his next books. The star in this firmament was to be a novel entitled *Answered Prayers*, a work that he loved to describe in detail to his editor Joe Fox and me over drinks and dinner whenever possible. This was to be an intricate, exuberant, witty, and mischievous novel, all told through the eyes of a never-to-be-forgotten character who in many ways reminded Truman of Truman himself. To use Truman's description, this was to be a kite with a long tail consisting of many chapters, some titles of which he whispered most confidentially into our easily seduced ears. Yes, he was writing away—yes, the fact is he had written at least half of the book—yes, it would soon be finished. . . . And the years rolled by and I renegotiated and revised the contracts. At times, there was hope. Three chapters were published in magazines. But then he gave us no more. At various times he assured us that it was all packed away and he was already in the editing stage, or it was almost all packed away, or some of it was packed away. And then he died.

I shall never forget the hours and hours and hours spent by me, Joe Fox, and Truman's biographer Gerald Clarke trying to find the rest of this momentous manuscript. We searched Truman's apartment, his house in Bridgehampton. We asked the people he had lived with. We tracked down the theories of well-meaning friends, all to no avail. And then we understood. There was no more. The great dissembler had simply fooled his closest friends and allies. There was no more because he simply could not write any more.

Although Joe is no longer here to testify, I am sure he would agree that we both felt cheated and somehow bruised but, who knows, perhaps in his delirium Truman really thought he had written the rest of this novel and locked it away and that his two godfathers, as he called us, would find it and bring it forward in all its glory.

Eventually Joe Fox suggested that the three chapters of *Answered Prayers* should be published in book form. He reasoned that all three had been published previously in magazines, that they were all well written, and that in some strange way they did manage to huddle together into a structure, if not cohesive then at least structurally sound. At the time I thought long and hard about this suggestion; after all, Truman had certainly not instructed Joe or me or anyone else to publish merely a first part of what was supposed to be a long novel. However, these pieces were Truman's last published writings, and in fact one of them, "La Côte Basque," a barely fictionalized description of some of Truman's closest celebrity friends, stood historically as a marker in Truman's subsequent downfall. It had proven too bloody for most of his friends to bear. Not only had they turned against him but by that time he had deteriorated to the point where he actually had turned against himself. We agreed that the book should be published, and it came out in 1987.

That decision turned out to be the easy one. A much more difficult decision arose late in 2004 and carried over to early 2005. In the fall of 2004 I received a letter from Sotheby's in New York stating that a trove of Capote memorabilia, including manuscripts of some published works, many letters, photographs, and what looked like an unpublished novel, had been delivered to Sotheby's for auction. None of us had any idea that these documents were in existence. Sotheby's indicated that an unknown person claimed that his uncle had been a house sitter at a basement apartment in Brooklyn

Heights that Truman had inhabited around 1950. He claimed
that Truman was away at one point but had decided not to
come back to the apartment and had instructed the superin-
tendent of the building to put all of his remaining possessions on the street for garbage pickup. According to this
account, when the house sitter saw what had been done, he
felt that he could not let this material be discarded, so he decided to keep it. Now, fifty years later, this gentleman had
died and a relative of his had come into possession of the material and wanted to sell it.

I realized immediately that Sotheby's was trying to get
me, as trustee of The Truman Capote Literary Trust, not
only to authenticate the material but also to acquiesce in its
sale. The catalogue Sotheby's sent listed the materials and
had photographs of some of them. Included was a photograph of a page or two of an unpublished manuscript from a
composition book Truman used for his writing.

My most reliable source for information about Truman
before I met him was his biographer Gerald Clarke. Not only
had Gerald written a luminous biography of Truman but he
also kept meticulous records about events in Truman's life.
In fact, Random House had just published a collection of
Truman's letters that were edited by Clarke and to which he
referred me. In those letters Truman writes of struggling

with this manuscript, a novel called *Summer Crossing*, for some time before finally putting it aside. Here the story varies. There is some evidence that he wished it never to be published, and yet in later letters to a friend there are also indications that he was still thinking about it. Truman never mentioned *Summer Crossing* to me nor did Gerald Clarke have a clear idea of what Truman's final wishes were for this manuscript. And Joe Fox had passed on in 1995.

Gerald Clarke went to see the material at Sotheby's and had a glimpse of the various items in the collection. There were in fact letters from Truman's mother and his stepfather (a rarity, and an insight into what we thought had been completely cutoff relationships). There were many, many letters to his beloved friend Newton Arvin, photographs of Truman as a young man, annotated manuscripts of some of Truman's early works, and, of course, what looked like a full manuscript of a novel entitled *Summer Crossing*.

The next step was to get a chance to read it. I asked David Ebershoff, who had taken over the editing chores of Truman's works at Random House, to arrange with Sotheby's to make a copy of the novel. While this was happening I had to be absolutely sure that if Sotheby's auctioned these documents they were to make very clear to all prospective purchasers that the publication rights belonged to The

Truman Capote Literary Trust and were not for sale as part of the documents. I also wanted to make sure, if at all possible, that all of these documents and memorabilia ended up in the place where Truman's other papers, manuscripts, and documents had been placed, namely the New York Public Library. I started a dialogue with the library and asked them to examine the material and hopefully arrange to buy it. Gerald Clarke also urged them to this end. In order to make sure that Sotheby's was going to clearly indicate that the publication rights belonged to The Truman Capote Literary Trust, I asked them to put flyers on every seat at the auction and also to make an announcement before the auction began that the only things being auctioned were the physical papers and that the publication rights belonged to the Trust. Just to make sure, I asked my son John Burnham Schwartz, a novelist in his own right and someone who knew Truman since he was a little boy, to check at Sotheby's to see that all was in order. The amazing conclusion to all of this was that apparently no one bid at the auction. This could have been for a couple of reasons. First, the price estimates were too high, and second, they were put off by the publication warnings we had arranged with Sotheby's.

Gerald Clarke, David Ebershoff, and I began a campaign to urge the New York Public Library to buy these documents and put them in the permanent Truman Capote Collection. Finally, an agreement was reached between Sotheby's and the library, and I am happy to say that the documents now safely reside with Truman's other papers for view by scholars and, in fact, anyone interested in literary history.

I read the manuscript of *Summer Crossing* with great excitement and a certain amount of dread. I remembered that it was quite likely that Truman did not want this novel to be published, but I was also hopeful that it would shed some light on Truman as a young author prior to the time he wrote his first iconic work, *Other Voices, Other Rooms*. Of course, I did not trust my own judgment. I therefore asked David Ebershoff and Robert Loomis, Truman's senior editor at Random House, as well as my wife, Louise, to read the manuscript and to share notes. It is fair to say that we were all happily surprised. While not a polished work, it fully reflects the emergence of an original voice and a surprisingly proficient writer of prose.

Of course, it was not for me alone to judge its literary merit. After much discussion, our verdict was that the manuscript should be published. We reasoned that this was a sufficiently mature work that could stand on its own merits and that its intimations of the later style and proficiency that led to *Breakfast at Tiffany's* were too valuable to be ignored.

Before making a final decision I asked my friend James Salter if he would take the responsibility of giving it one more read. Not only is Jim a good friend but he is generally recognized as one of the most luminous prose stylists of my generation. Jim graciously accepted the task and after a short while told me that he concurred in the verdict of my other three judges more or less for the same reasons. The decision was then up to me.

As a lawyer, I realize more than most the responsibilities of a trustee of a charitable trust. I am also very conscious of the high standard of care that any fiduciary must apply in reaching his or her decisions. However, it is not often that a trustee or even a literary executor is put into a position where he must decide whether to publish a work of an important deceased author that, very likely, the author would not have published in his lifetime. Truman died in 1984. What would he have thought now? Would he have had the historical perspective and indeed the clearheadedness to decide what was best for the manuscript? After much thought it became apparent to me that in the final analysis the novel had to speak for itself. Although it was imperfect, its surprising literary merits seemed to demand an escape from its previous captivity. It would be published.

I wish to thank my advisors and everyone else who has

helped make this publication happen. At the end of the day, of course, the responsibility for this decision, legally, ethically, and aesthetically, is and must be mine alone. In this I am mindful of the ironic twist of fate that prevented us from publishing a novel Truman believed he had finished (*Answered Prayers*) but allows us to publish this novel, which most likely he did not want published. As I write this I see Truman with his impish grin wagging a finger at me. "You are a naughty avvocato!" he is saying. But he is smiling.

ALAN U. SCHWARTZ

October 2005

A Note on the Text

This first edition of *Summer Crossing* was set from Capote's manuscript, which was written in four school notebooks with sixty-two pages of supplemental notes, archived in the New York Public Library's Truman Capote collection. The editors have silently corrected any inconsistent usages and misspellings. In instances when the author's meaning was not clear, the editors added punctuation such as a comma, and in a few sentences, when a word was missing, the editors have inserted it. The editors' foremost concern has been to faithfully reproduce the author's manuscript. They made their corrections solely for the purpose of clarifying the unclear.

The Truman Capote Papers
at the New York Public Library

The manuscript of *Summer Crossing* consists of four note-books written in ink and heavily corrected in Capote's hand. The manuscript is supplemented by sixty-two pages of notes. The manuscript and notes make up part of the Truman Capote Papers housed in the Manuscripts and Archives Division of the New York Public Library's Humanities and Social Sciences Library. The majority of the papers were donated by the Capote estate to the New York Public Library in 1985; subsequent purchases have been made by the library to supplement the collection, including the manuscript of *Summer Crossing*.

The Truman Capote Papers consist of holograph manu-

scripts and typescripts of the author's published and unpublished work, notes and other material related to the works,
Capote's high school writings, correspondence, photographs,
graphic materials, miscellaneous personal documents, printed
material, and scrapbooks.

The Manuscripts and Archives Division holds archival
material in over three thousand collections, dating from the
third millennium BCE to the current decade. The greatest
strengths of the division are the papers and records of individuals, families, and organizations, primarily from the New
York region. These collections, dating from the eighteenth
through the twentieth centuries, support research in the po-
litical, economic, social, and cultural history of New York
and the United States. Notable collections include the
records of *The New Yorker,* Macmillan Publishing Company,
National Audubon Society, the New York World's Fairs, and
papers of individuals as diverse as Thomas Jefferson, Lillian
Wald, H. L. Mencken, and Robert Moses.

ABOUT THE TYPE

This book is set in Fournier, a typeface named for Pierre Simon Fournier, the youngest son of a French printing family. He started out engraving woodblocks and large capitals, then moved on to fonts of type. In 1736 he began his own foundry and made several important contributions in the field of type design; he is said to have cut 147 alphabets of his own creation. Fournier is probably best remembered as the designer of St. Augustine Ordinaire, a face that served as the model for Monotype's Fournier, which was released in 1925.